RELUCTANT SHOWDOWN

"Johnny, why don't you stand up real slowlike and let me see your sidearm."

Sonora's smile disappeared. "It can't be like that, Ray."

"You want a fair fight?"

The outlaw nodded. "In the street."

"Let's go."

They marched into the tiny dirt street of Manteca. Windows and doors slammed shut in the little village. A few passersby ran for cover. Cracks were left in curtains so curious eyes could watch the showdown.

"I don't want to kill you, Ray. But like I said, you ain't the kind to quit."

The big man felt a cold sweat breaking all over him.

Sonora hung his hand by his side. "You draw first, Ray."

Raider's gut was churning. Sweat dripped into his eyes. He went for his Peacemaker, but like before, he never saw the kid's hand move. Johnny Sonora beat him to the punch. . . .

RAIDER

THE CALIFORNIA KID

J.D. HARDIN

BERKLEY BOOKS, NEW YORK

THE CALIFORNIA KID

A Berkley Book/published by arrangement with
the author

PRINTING HISTORY
Berkley edition/March 1990

ISBN: 0-425-12011-2

This book is dedicated to
Jamie and Peter, two good guys.

Also to Charlie of the Northland.

THE
CALIFORNIA KID

CHAPTER ONE

Raider reined back the tall pinto gelding, easing to a stop along the trail that ran the edge of Yainax Butte. He was a good two day ride east of Klamath Falls, Oregon, in pursuit of an outlaw named Charlie Pawpaw. Pawpaw had stolen a strongbox from a Wells Fargo coach that had been heading north from California to Seattle. The coach company had been carrying ten thousand dollars of its own money, mostly in scrip paper, some of it in gold. All of the money had been hidden in the lockbox, which was purloined by a man who was riding shotgun and had, until that time, been a loyal employee of the Wells Fargo company. Now he was just another robber that the tall Pinkerton had been enlisted to apprehend.

The pinto snorted, tossing its head.

Raider patted the animal's neck. "You been workin' too hard t' catch this one, boy. Just like me."

The big man dismounted, peering out over the rugged valley below him. Foul mists and wispy clouds swelled threateningly under a gray, foreboding sky. Oregon weather could get pretty lousy in a hurry. Raider had been wearing a slicker to stave off the cold, hateful drizzle. Even with the slicker to cover his muscular frame, he still felt damp and rheumatic. His cotton shirt and denim pants needed to be hung over a fire to dry, along with his soggy socks and his long johns. The black Stetson drooped over his forehead and his boots were loose. He just wanted to catch Charlie Pawpaw and get it over with.

Raider's black eyes scanned the valley for movement through the mist. He had picked up Pawpaw's trail in Chiloquin. A store-keeper had described the short, red-faced man who wore a dark blue derby. The man had stopped to buy a saddle blanket for his mule. He had also been traveling with a squaw, a fact that gave Raider hope. A woman would slow him down. The storekeeper had not been able to determine the tribe of the squaw, but he remarked that Pawpaw must be pretty fond of her. He bought her a calico dress and had paid with gold.

A mosquito whined in front of Raider's rugged face. When the insect landed on his beard, he slapped it dead. The damned bugs in Oregon were unbearable sometimes, especially at night. He remembered the joke about mosquitos carrying off a grizzly bear to hide it so the big mosquitos wouldn't take it away from them. Maybe the story was true, after all.

"Damn you, Charlie Pawpaw."

The pinto snorted. Raider fished in his saddlebags until he found the half-full oat bag. He slipped it over the animal's ears so the gelding could eat. Then he gazed back into the mist, wonder-ing if Pawpaw had really come this way.

From Chiloquin, Raider had followed the outlaw's trail along the shore of a big lake. Pawpaw headed south for a while, riding his mule and trailing two horses behind him. At first Raider had figured the trail was leading straight to Klamath Falls. But then Pawpaw had taken a left turn, heading east toward the hills. Maybe he knew somebody was on his trail. Hell, how could a man steal that much money and not expect somebody to come after him? Maybe Pawpaw was planning to run in circles; head into the wooded areas, traipse around, and then turn back to Bonanza or Klamath Falls.

Raider slapped another mosquito. "Damned varmints."

He wished that the sun would break through the clouds. He hadn't really seen much sign of the fleeing bandit, not since he had left the lakeshore.

The pinto shook its head, telling him that the oat bag was empty. Raider felt empty himself. When he put the feeder in his saddlebag, he searched for some dried meat for himself, finally coming up with a crusty stick of beef. Not much, but enough to fill the hole in his belly.

When he had swallowed the last bite, he decided to check his weapons. His Colt hung low on his hip. Raider drew it and spun the cylinder. He had loaded five slugs, leaving the hammer on an empty chamber. The gun needed oil, so he used the small bottle in his saddlebag, dousing the iron and the redwood handle. The revolver hadn't started to rust yet and it wouldn't, if he kept it primed.

His rifle was another story. To keep the rust from creeping up the barrel of the Winchester, he had to wrap it in oilcloth. That precaution meant that he wouldn't be able to wield it as quickly from the scabbard on his sling ring.

Raider took a deep breath of damp air. He had ascended to the top of the butte to see if he could get a better look at the surrounding area. He wondered how well Charlie Pawpaw knew Oregon. One of the Wells Fargo men had claimed that the outlaw was from Spokane, but there was no way to be sure. Pawpaw had probably been lying all along, working diligently for the company, waiting until he had the right chance to steal a big stash of money.

He had gotten his chance. He had also killed the two men who were working with him, as well as the two passengers on the coach, which meant he had to be quick and sneaky. According to the Wells Fargo company, one of the men supposedly had been Pawpaw's best friend. Raider had to give it to the lawbreaker. The plan had required a great deal of patience and calculation. Unless Pawpaw had done it on the spur of the moment, acting without thinking. Either way, Raider figured to be careful if he got close to the man.

But that didn't seem likely. He had lost the trail and it appeared that ascending to the top of the rise had been a mistake. All he could see was mist and patches of green. He rubbed his mustache, peering down into the valley. Hell, he had to catch up to Pawpaw. The outlaw was traveling with a woman and that meant he had to slow down, even if she was a squaw.

What the hell was he doing with the woman anyway? Had he picked her up along the trail? Maybe she had been in on the act. Raider wasn't sure. The Wells Fargo investigators had found the coach abandoned, with the crew and passengers dead. What had caused them to stop? And how the hell had Pawpaw gotten the drop on them?

He turned back to the pinto. "Looks like this might be a long one, boy. You ready to ride?"

The pinto snorted when he swung into the saddle. Raider hated to backtrack but he didn't have much choice. He had to pick up a trail somewhere.

As he made for the trail that led down off the butte, the sun tried to peek through the clouds, a momentary sliver of warmth and light. Raider started to take off the slicker but the sun fled as quickly as it had come. The misty drizzle held steady, suspended in the air rather than falling. Mosquitos hovered in front of his nose, waiting for the right moment to strike. Raider took off his limp Stetson and brushed them away.

"Hateful weather for a manhunt," he said to himself.

He tried to form a plan. Come down, make it to Bonanza, ask around about Pawpaw. Maybe the outlaw really was from the area. Maybe he had a hideout into the hills, a place in the trees where he could hole up with the squaw until everybody had forgotten about him.

Raider entertained notions that only came when he was tired and cold and wet. The idea of hiding in the mountains somewhere seemed good to him. Hell, mountain men were the only ones left with any true freedom. Cities and towns seemed to be popping up everywhere these days. Why, a man couldn't ride for more than a week without seeing somebody or some settlement. Not like his younger days. With the silver boom and the land rush, men were flocking to the west with high hopes and dreams.

When he reached the trail that led back into the valley, he had to dismount and walk the pinto. It was a good mount. A man in Gulley Wash, Colorado, had sold it to him for a paltry ten dollars. The pinto had a sore on its right foreleg, which made it a little lame at first. But some sulphur powder and a little fish grease had healed the wound and now the animal was running better than a fresh colt. The brown-and-white gelding had served him as good as any mount he could remember.

"It won't be long boy, I—"

He stopped still on the trail, gazing down into the mists again. From his vantage point he could see the trees that lay to the southwest. Something seemed to be moving in the billows of fog.

"Son of a bitch."

He heard the echoes of the moving horses. Three of them. Then the man's voice came behind the noise of the animals. Moving west, probably doubling back to Klamath Falls.

Maybe it wasn't Charlie Pawpaw.

Raider squinted, trying to make out the shapes.

The braying of a mule came over the air, as if it was close by, but the figures in the distance were probably two miles away. They dipped into the mist again, hidden from Raider's view, until the sun broke through for a moment. Then he saw the woman's calico dress. She was sitting on one of the trailing horses. It was Charlie Pawpaw and his squaw. Raider just hoped he would be able to get down off the butte in time to catch them.

CHAPTER TWO

All was not well at the Pinkerton National Detective Agency. William Wagner sat at his desk in the Fifth Avenue offices of the company, nervously wiping his wire-rimmed spectacles. He had just received a disturbing telegram from an agent in Lincoln, Nebraska. It was the kind of trouble that Allan Pinkerton hated.

"William!"

Wagner put on his spectacles and gazed in the direction of the hulking Scotsman. Pinkerton had come out of his office to catch Wagner in a reverie. They stared at each other for a few seconds.

Pinkerton gestured to the telegram in Wagner's hand. "Trouble?"

Wagner nodded. "From one of our men in Nebraska."

"The silo murders?"

"Yes."

Pinkerton waved slightly with his hand. "We'd better discuss this in private. Hurry along."

Wagner joined his supervisor in Pinkerton's neat office. He took a seat on the other side of the huge oak desk, refusing a cup of coffee. Pinkerton poured himself a cup of the steaming black liquid and eased into his soft leather chair.

"The telegram, William. What does it say?"

Wagner eyed the terse message. "Well, it seems that Avery caught the man who had murdered those farm workers. Only, he had to kill the culprit and now he's being held for murder himself."

"Hmm."

Wagner hesitated, watching Pinkerton as he considered the possibilities.

Finally the big Scotsman held forth. "Who hired us on this one?"

"One of the farmers."

"Hmm." Pinkerton looked up at the ceiling. "Not good. It would have been better had we been workin' with the local law boys."

Wagner sighed deeply. "For once that would have been a blessing."

"Is anyone else with Avery?"

Wagner shook his head. "No."

"Send Stokes immediately, as soon as you can get out a wire. Have him find a lawbook thumper and see that Avery gets a fair trial."

"Maybe there's something else we can do," Wagner offered.

"Such as?"

Wagner leaned forward a little. "Well, perhaps we could have the trial moved to another town. Let the state authorities intervene. You know how local sentiment can run. What if the killer happened to be related to members of the jury? Why, I—"

Pinkerton cut him off, nodding appreciatively. "Yes, I see what you mean. I don't like this kind of trouble, William."

"I know, sir."

Pinkerton exhaled defeatedly. "We have to talk about some unpleasant things now, William."

"Yes, I am aware of that."

"If we have to go in and get Avery ourselves, it might be sticky."

"To say the least," Wagner rejoined.

"Where's Raider?"

That seemed like the logical response to a forceful issue. If Avery was innocent, Pinkerton was not going to let him hang. And Raider would be the one to send into that sort of ruckus.

"Well?" Pinkerton urged. "Where is he?"

"Northwest," Wagner replied.

"Washington? Idaho?"

Wagner shrugged. "Maybe. Or Oregon, maybe California. He's chasing some outlaw called Charlie Pawpaw."

Pinkerton put his hands together, resting them on his stomach. "Well, let's hope it doesn't come to that. And by the way, William, we never talked about it, not officially."

"I understand."

"Get word to Raider anyway."

Wagner nodded. "I'll try. But you know how he operates. We may not hear from him for months."

"Do your best, William. Do your best."

Wagner took the cue for his retreat. Pinkerton wanted to be alone, to study the situation further. One of his men was in trouble and he had to get him out. The reputation of the agency was also on the line, as always.

Wagner closed the door behind him. He had to get several messages to the Western Union office. It was going to take time to get things rolling. In the meantime, he'd have to hope for a wire from Raider.

It was a hope that would go in vain.

But Wagner persisted with the endeavor. He wished there was a faster, more efficient way to handle his affairs. As it stood, he would have to settle for a quick wire message and a little bit of bad luck.

CHAPTER THREE

Raider peered south, watching Charlie Pawpaw and the woman as they made their way along the narrow path. What the hell was he going to do? Standing right there, staring at his quarry, he had no way of stopping them. He reached for the Winchester, taking it out of the scabbard, unrolling the oilcloth. Out of frustration, he jacked a cartridge into the chamber, sending a metallic echo through the damp air.

He froze with the rifle in hand. What if Pawpaw heard the echo? Raider watched to see if the outlaw turned back to look at him. Pawpaw just kept going, probably heading for Klamath Falls.

Raider drew a bead on the distant figures, which looked like June bugs crawling across a summer lawn. One shot. Hell, it wouldn't reach them but he still wanted to pull the trigger. Let Pawpaw know there was somebody on his ass. Scare him into making a mistake.

He lowered the rifle and began to wrap it in the oilcloth. No sense ruining his chance for a surprise. Pawpaw didn't seem to be in any particular hurry, although he wasn't lagging either. He dropped the rifle into the scabbard and looked down again.

The outlaw and his woman were turning a bend, disappearing

into the mist. Why the hell had Pawpaw doubled back this way in the first place? Maybe he had kin in the mountains. Maybe he was dropping off his treasure, hiding it where it would be safe.

Raider patted the pinto on the neck. "Let's go get him, boy. An' try not t' make too much of a ruckus. I don't want him t' hear us till it's too late."

The descent took too long. By the time he was back in the valley, Raider could no longer hear Pawpaw and the woman. When he finally found the trail that led west, he turned to gaze north for a few seconds. Where the hell had Pawpaw been coming from? Was there another path that led down from Chiloquin? Raider considered retracing Pawpaw's steps but then figured it was better to catch the outlaw and ask him firsthand. Of course, there was always the chance that Pawpaw would not be taken alive. Raider had never known a corpse to give up too many answers.

He started west, leading the pinto. The trail was too uneven and rocky to risk riding the broad-shouldered animal. Raider wanted him ready to run when he needed a fast horse.

Pawpaw left a wide trail that was easy to follow. Almost too easy. Which meant that he was probably unaware of Raider's presence behind him. Still, even with Raider's new fortunes, Pawpaw had at least a three hour head start. Even if he was riding with three horses and carrying a woman along, a skillful traveler could keep the distance between them. Raider had to go twice as fast to make up the difference, which meant wearing out his mount and himself.

If the outlaw made it to Klamath Falls before Raider, he might be able to grab a stagecoach south to California or north to Portland. That would make the search a lot tougher, especially if Raider had to come back to Oregon to look for the stashed money. No, it was better if he caught Pawpaw soon. Then he could get the hell out of the wet northwest.

He slapped another mosquito.

A rumble triggered overhead as gray clouds billowed up against the sky in front of him.

He pulled his hat down over his eyes, waiting for the rain as he plodded steadily to the south.

• • •

The rain never hit the big man from Arkansas. Instead, the clouds rolled past him, never dropping their payload. The sun came out just long enough to fall back into the horizon. The bugs woke up and the other creatures pushed out of their dens to roam the dark woods.

As Raider was bemoaning the onset of night, the land leveled out a little, allowing him to ride again. The pinto seemed ready. Cool air rushed by his face as the gelding began to cover long stretches of ground.

Raider felt better about his chances. Even though his pace in the mountains had been the same as Pawpaw's, there was no way the outlaw could move on open ground as quickly as a lone horseman. Pawpaw could run, but he'd have to make allowances for the load he was carrying. Pack horses just couldn't gallop as fast as the pinto.

The darkness made it harder to track, but at least the rain had stopped for a while. A full moon had begun to make its way into the sky and the Oregon night didn't seem to be that much colder than the day.

Not a bad night to chase somebody. He could see the trail pretty well. In fact, when he rode up on the dead packhorse, he recognized what it was immediately.

He reined back on the pinto, which snorted and reared at the smell of fresh blood. Raider dismounted and held tightly to the reins of the skittish pinto as he bent to touch the body of the packhorse. It wasn't warm but it hadn't really started to stiffen yet. A pretty fresh kill. Probably had taken up lame, forcing Pawpaw to shoot it.

The big man frowned. He hadn't heard a shot. He touched the animal's neck, feeling for a wound. He found the trench left behind by a sharp knife. The horse had died slowly, its heart pumping out the last of its blood.

Raider stood up, gazing south. Why hadn't Pawpaw shot the lame animal or left it to hobble? Maybe he knew somebody was after him and he didn't want to make a noise. He could've been the cheap kind, just wanting to save a bullet. Had he watched the slowly dying creature?

Raider shook his head, sucking for air.

The pinto snorted. It wanted to be away from the smell of blood. Raider couldn't blame the gelding. He wasn't much on the remains that death left behind. The sight made his stomach turn and his spine seemed to be crawling with red ants.

Swinging into the saddle, he urged the pinto to the west. Charlie Pawpaw couldn't be too far away. The dead packhorse was proof of that. Raider felt good having the pinto underneath him. A strong, fast mount made a difference—something that Charlie Pawpaw was going to find out.

He held steady until he saw the light of the campfire burning on the trail ahead of him. It came up all of a sudden, flashing at him between the trees. He had to stop the gelding and dismount quickly. Had Pawpaw heard him approaching?

He damned Oregon under his breath. He hated chasing men through thick forests. On the open plain, you could see a camp-fire five or ten miles away. Raider doubted that he was a quarter mile away from the flickering flames and shadows of this fire.

No sounds. No voices. Then something clanked, but everything fell silent again. Raider hesitated with his hand on his Colt. Maybe it was a trap. Or maybe it wasn't even the man he was chasing.

He tied the pinto and then drew his revolver. Best to have a closer look. Determine if the campers were Pawpaw and his squaw. Then take measures to stop them and take them alive if possible.

Easing through the brush, he kept low, listening. A damned quiet night. Too quiet. The pinto nickered behind him.

Raider froze, watching the fire, which was a hundred feet away. If he could hear the pinto then they could hear it too. Still no sign of movement in the camp.

He heard more horses nickering in response to the pinto. Rustling sounds. Shadows seemed to move in the light of the fire. A man stood up suddenly, staring straight at Raider who crouched in the shadows.

The big Pinkerton expected gunfire but it didn't come right away.

The man moved in the shadows again. Raider caught a glimpse of the derby, which appeared dark blue in the firelight. Pawpaw.

Raider thumbed back the hammer of the Colt.

Had Pawpaw seen him?

His heart tried to escape through his throat. Sweat breaking in the cool air. Eyes darting back and forth. Keep his senses honed. Don't let Pawpaw get off the first shot.

What the hell had the outlaw heard anyway? The approach of another rider. But it probably didn't matter who approached; if Pawpaw was carrying a lot of his stolen loot, he'd be wary of any stranger.

Raider started through the brush. It didn't matter now. He was going to take Pawpaw as best he could. And he really didn't expect the outlaw to cooperate at all.

The gates of Hell seemed to open up as Raider approached the edge of the camp. A woman screamed and a pistol exploded twice. Raider saw the muzzle flashes, firing twice himself, blasting the Colt in the general direction of the gunshots.

The horses snorted from the shadows.

Raider leaped over the fire, peering into the darkness at the rim of the flame's light. "Give it up, Charlie."

Hooves moved behind him.

Raider whirled to fire again. Something clipped him from the right, knocking the gun from his hand. A horse's flank rushed by, finishing the job, knocking the big Pinkerton into the campfire.

Raider scuffled to his feet, brushing the red coals off his jeans. When he was in no danger of burning to death, he bent over, feeling the ground for his Colt. By the time he found the gun, the hoofbeats of the departing mount were no longer audible in the still night.

He fired two shots after Pawpaw, just to make sure he wasn't hiding in the shadows. Fat chance. He just fired to make himself feel better. He had come so close.

"Damn!"

Keeping the smoking pistol in hand, Raider began to search the camp. The woman had cried out just before Pawpaw fired his pistol, which meant that she was probably in bad shape. The outlaw figured to rid himself of his burden with a couple of quick shots. Pawpaw had heard Raider and wasn't looking to take any chances, not with a lot of money on him.

Raider stumbled over the body that was clad in calico. He peered down with the moon shining over his shoulder. Pawpaw had covered the squaw's head with a blanket before he shot her. The hole in the blanket was smoking, seared by the exploding powder. A thick, red ooze spread out from the hole. No need to look to see if she was dead.

He turned back in the direction of his own mount. He could

bury the woman later. Stay after Pawpaw, even in the dark. Keep coming, like a wounded wolf or a bear at a watering hole. Make the outlaw think that Satan himself was on his tail.

Instead of daybreak, Raider got another bank of rain clouds that rolled in from the northwest. He had ridden through the night, finding numerous signs of Pawpaw on the trail. In his haste, the fugitive was leaving behind a path that could easily be followed by the light of the moon.

Pawpaw had turned due north, making for Chiloquin. Raider was almost sure he would try to intercept the lakeshore at some point. Maybe try to find a boat to get away in.

Raider pressed on in the rain. He had to catch Pawpaw before he got to the lake. And he seemed to be getting closer. Pawpaw's mount was leaving deep holes in the fresh, dark mud.

Hadn't the outlaw been riding a mule? Raider tried to remember what had run past him in the dark. Hadn't it been a horse that had knocked him down? Too fuzzy to remember. He had never really gotten a look at Pawpaw's mount as it carried the short man to freedom.

Raider slowed the pinto when the trail widened. He came down a short slope of barren rock and reined up at the bank of the lake. The water stretched out to a blank, foggy horizon. If Pawpaw had gotten a boat, he could be halfway to Klamath Falls by nightfall.

Something caught Raider's eyes. A flash of white at the water's edge. At first he thought it was foam; then he realized the object was floating in the lake, bouncing against the shoreline.

Dismounting, he fished the white ring from the water and examined it. A ring of carved bone with a couple of feathers attached to it. Something that an Indian woman would have made for herself, maybe to wear in her hair. Had Pawpaw taken the trinket as a memento, only to throw it away after second thoughts?

The pinto snorted, rearing.

Raider figured the animal wanted to drink so he pulled it down to the edge of the water. The pinto nosed for a second but then raised its head, looking to the right.

"What are you onto?"

He gazed in the same direction, looking for signs on the narrow trail. Too much rain for tracks. He decided to tie up the gelding and have a look on foot.

Ankle-deep in water, he sloshed forward with his hand on his Colt. He wanted to keep it under his slicker until the last minute. No need to expose it to the rain unless it was necessary.

The forest along the lakeshore was almost as thick as the valley where he had been earlier. Winding through the trees, he kept his eyes wide, darting from side to side. The rain came down harder, making his ears useless in the din of the downpour.

He was close. He knew it. Keep going forward. Pawpaw was slowing down. Hadn't counted on a Pinkerton who could chase him through anything.

Raider stopped when he saw the brown shapes ahead of him, blurred by the wall of Oregon rain. He knew there was a horse tied to a tree. And the other shape seemed to be a man hunkered down by the ground.

His back was turned to Raider. The big man doubted if Pawpaw could hear him in the rain. The horse might snort, but it would be too late.

Raider drew the Colt and started forward. When he got close enough, he could see the dark blue derby. Pawpaw was hunched over, like he was trying to start a fire.

The mount made a fuss, but the derby never budged.

Raider reached over, grabbing the outlaw's shoulder. He spun the body around and pointed the Colt at a placid, brown face.

The big man's eyes bulged. "You!"

The squaw laughed at him. She giggled hard as he dropped her into the mud. Pawpaw had tricked him. Staged the whole thing. Dressed the squaw in his own clothes when he knew Raider was closing in. Then he faked the hole in the blanket, had probably killed his own packhorse to get the blood he needed to top off the deception. He had figured that Raider wouldn't look under the blanket if the blood was thick enough.

And what if the big man had decided to peek under the blanket? Pawpaw would have raised up with a shotgun or a pistol, probably blowing Raider to the gates of St. Peter. A clever bastard if ever there was one.

The woman was trying to get up out of the mud.

Raider turned to see her rushing at him with a knife in hand. He caught her wrist and sent her sprawling again. Pawpaw had given her orders to kill the big man in the slicker.

Why hadn't he seen it coming? Because he didn't look under the blanket. Finally some good luck on a bad day. He hadn't captured Pawpaw, but he was still alive to try again.

A shiver rolled over his shoulders. For a moment, he felt sick in his gut, like he wanted to heave out all the anger inside him. But he shook it off and started for the pinto. He had to go back and pick up the trail again.

The woman ran behind him, screaming at the top of her lungs. Raider wheeled back and fired twice over her head, putting a stopper on her enthusiasm. She would be better off forgetting about Charlie Pawpaw. Raider still planned to see the outlaw swinging from a rope or lying in a pine box. Dead men don't make good husbands.

By late afternoon, Raider was back at the encampment where he had flushed out Charlie Pawpaw. He had to appreciate the trick—dressing the woman like a man, making her ride out, leading the pursuer away while he lay under the blanket. A trick to remember and use one day.

The blanket was lying there on the wet ground, the bloody bullet hole staring up like a jaundiced eye. Pawpaw's calling card. A hateful reminder that Raider had been careless, even if the carelessness had saved his life in the final bargain.

Raider sifted through the debris left behind by Pawpaw but didn't find anything too revealing. He wondered if the outlaw had fled in the calico dress he had worn for the blanket ruse.

The big man slapped his hands together. It was a great trick, even if it had been played on him. Pawpaw had even made sure his mule was there, leaving the squaw to ride out on the other packhorse. If Raider had gotten a good look at the fleeing animal, he might have—

He shook off the second thoughts. Best not to worry about it. Just keep on, try to figure what Pawpaw would do. Probably head to Klamath Falls, Raider thought.

He took a deep breath, thinking that he should sleep some before he rode west again. If Klamath Falls was it. What if Pawpaw headed for the California border? It didn't matter. Raider was going to Klamath Falls.

He rode west, hoping he would intersect some trail that he could be certain would lead him into Klamath Falls. He was ready to give up and sleep some when the pinto died on him. It just stopped cold and fell into the mud. A hell of a thing to happen when the rain was just getting started.

So Raider pulled off the saddle and found a high spot on a slope above the trail. He propped up the saddle, climbing under it, cradling his rifle to his belly like a slender woman. Nothing in the world mattered to the big man from Arkansas. He only wanted to close his eyes, to sleep or maybe to die. It didn't make much difference to him; either way, he would be unconscious.

CHAPTER FOUR

William Wagner slammed his fist on the desk, an uncharacteristic display of impatience from the bespectacled ramrod of the Pinkerton National Detective Agency. For an entire day he had been sending messages by Western Union, only to have all replies come back negative. Not one of his agents had seen Stokes or Raider. Even the men who were working in the same territory had drawn blanks when it came to the whereabouts of either agent.

Wagner knew he shouldn't have been so angry at the fact that he could not find two of his men. It was quite common for him to go weeks and months before he heard from agents on the job. His irritation came from the fact that another agent was in trouble. He wouldn't rest until justice had been done for P. W. Avery.

Pinkerton agents had been accused of crimes before. Sometimes the locals weren't too happy about an outsider, especially when the outsider brought one of their own citizens to trial for a crime he had committed. Railroad justice, however unappealing, still existed in the west. Wagner just hoped that Avery could be saved from the indigenous lynch mob.

The front door of the office opened, diverting Wagner's attention from his troubles. He lifted his eyes to the man who deliv-

21

ered the morning mail. There wouldn't be anything about Stokes
or Raider in the post. There hadn't been enough time to dispatch
a letter. After all, he had only started searching for them the day
before.

Still, to keep his mind off circumstances beyond his immedi-
ate control, he decided to search through the packets for anything
of interest. His gaze fixed on a brown dispatch from Lincoln,
Nebraska, the place where P. W. Avery was being held. He
opened the package to find a local newspaper called the *Lincoln
Free Sentinel*.

After reading the banner headline, he stood up behind his
desk. "My God!" He knew he had to show the paper to his supe-
rior.

Pinkerton was behind his desk, starting on his second pot of
coffee. He looked up when Wagner burst in without knocking.
"I've never known ya to be short on manners, William."

Wagner threw the paper in front of him. "Read the headline."

Pinkerton lifted it into his range of vision. "Pinkerton Agent to
be Tried for Murder."

The big Scotsman shrugged. "We knew this already."

"Read on."

Pinkerton's eyes returned to the page. After a few moments,
he stood up and cried out. "Good Lord. It says they're gonna try
him as soon as the circuit judge comes from Omaha."

"Yes, I know."

Pinkerton's face slacked into a helpless frown. "It says here
that the judge is expected in three weeks. But the paper is—"

"Two weeks old," Wagner replied. "That means our man will
probably go on trial next week."

Pinkerton sat down again, letting out a deep sigh. "And I'm
guessin' there's no word from Stokes."

"Nor Raider."

Pinkerton turned a wary expression on his associate. "First
things first. Do we have anyone else around here? Someone that
could at least go to Nebraska and find a lawyer for Avery?"

Wagner lifted his chin proudly. "I thought I would go in per-
son. I think I can get to Lincoln in a week."

"And we've tried messages to the local lawmen?"

Wagner nodded. "But I think somebody has it for our man.
Read there in the paper. See what the local sheriff says?"

Pinkerton perused the page for a few more seconds. "Yes. He thinks he has Avery red-handed."

Wagner cleared his throat. "Now, I know we feel differently, but I think it's time we considered the possibility that Avery may have dealt his own hand in this thing."

"I don't care!" Pinkerton replied. "Guilty or innocent, I want him to at least have his say in court. And no backwoods judge is going to push him around either. He gets a fair trial."

"I agree wholeheartedly."

Pinkerton waved him toward the door. "Go on, William. Get yourself ready. You'll need to leave as soon as possible. Take the train as far as you can and then hire a private coach if need be."

Wagner nodded and started to turn away.

"William!"

Wagner hesitated, gazing at his boss's serious expression. "Yes, sir?"

"Don't let 'em bully you! Understand?"

Wagner tried to smile. "I won't."

He left Pinkerton's office, compiling a list of things he had to do: First, a train south; then a stagecoach, maybe a horse. Pinkerton had given him the authorization to use a private coach, something the old man rarely did. It showed the seriousness of the trouble. One week to save an agent's neck.

Wagner just hoped he was in time.

CHAPTER FIVE

The damned pinto just kept dying under him. It would crumble and fall and Raider hit the dirt over and over, repeating like a fast-cranked Winchester. He kept telling himself that he had not ridden the animal too hard. No harder than he had driven himself in search of Charlie Pawpaw.

What the hell was a pawpaw anyway?

Each time the pinto died, he heard the horrible snapping of bone, the thud of a ton of horseflesh falling in the mud.

There was a song from his childhood, echoing through his head: "Pickin' up pawpaws, put 'em in your pocket." Pawpaws fell out of trees. Charlie had fallen out of sight.

The damned pinto hadn't held up. It was his fault for riding it too long without a rest. Once again he heard in his mind the snapping bones, the last rattle of breath from the horse, and saw himself flying into the mud.

Then he felt something in his ribs, prodding him. It felt like the barrel of a rifle. Somebody getting the drop on him. Only it was real, like Charlie Pawpaw had doubled back to get him.

Raider cried out and lurched forward. Something stopped him from falling down the slope. He opened his eyes, fleeing from the nightmare of the dying pinto and the rifle barrel in his ribs.

25

Only the rifle was in front of him. And his own hand was full of his Colt. It was pointed at the man who held the rifle, an old single-shot breech loader. Raider had awakened to a standoff.

The rifleman backed away. "Whoa, big 'un. No need for iron."

Raider focused on the seedy figure of the intruder. A poor man by any observation. Felt hat, faded and drooping from the rain. Tattered slicker and worn pants. Holes in his boots. The rifle was rusty, making Raider wonder if it would even fire.

He shifted out from under the saddle. "Why're you sneakin' up on me like that, honcho?"

The man shrugged. "That your dead horse down there in the road?"

"What if it is?"

"I don't know. I just saw it. Then I seen you up here sleepin'. Thought you might need a hand."

Raider's eyes narrowed. He ached to believe the man, but he knew that the man wanted something. A trade or a barter. But what the hell did Raider have to offer in such a sorry state?

"You live around these parts?" the big man asked.

The felt hat nodded up and down. "Yes, I reckon I do. Headed for Klamath Falls just now. You need a ride? I got a wagon."

A scowl from the wet, aching Pinkerton. "You wouldn't shoot me in the back if I went to sleep?"

The man frowned since his dignity had been called into question. "Hey, pardner, I coulda kilt you just now while you were out cold. Wouldn't have been a hard shot."

That made sense to Raider. "Yeah, I reckon you could've. So you just want to give me a ride to Klamath Falls?"

The man shifted a little on his feet, looking away. "Well, that's part of it. I would ask one thing of you, though."

"I knew it."

"It ain't much."

Raider waved the barrel of his Colt. "Go on, spill it."

The man pointed back toward the road. "I want you to sell me that pinto. Give you five dollars for it."

Raider grimaced. "You mean all you want from me is that damned dead pony?"

"Nothin' more."

"And you'll give me five dollars?"

The man exhaled. "All right, I'll give you six. But that's all I can give you for it."

Raider still wasn't ready to relinquish his drop on the ratty character. "What the hell you want a damned dead horse for?"

"Well," the stranger replied, "I can skin him out. Horse hide is always worth somethin'. And there's the hooves. My wife makes glue out of 'em. Then there's the meat."

Raider shuddered. He hated horse meat, though he had eaten it on several unfortunate occasions. Some swore by it though and often preferred it to a good cut of beef.

"See," the man went on, "I can sell it in Klamath Falls and Chiloquin. Ain't much cattle raisin' up this way. Most of our beef up here comes from California, down Stockton way. Ain't really got a rail into this part of Oregon yet so I bring meat into both towns sometimes. It's a way to make a little money. Only I ain't been able to find any beef hereabouts, not lately anyway. So that pinto will do fine. Ain't even been dead a whole day yet."

Raider had heard enough. He felt the man in the floppy hat was no longer a threat. As he holstered his Colt, he realized that it had stopped raining. The air was fresh and clear, although clouds still covered the sky overhead.

"What day is it?" he asked the man.

"I ain't sure," came the reply.

"Okay, what time of day is it?"

The man grinned. "Why, it's mornin'," he replied proudly.

He had slept through the night. The sleep hadn't helped much. His body was still hurting from fatigue. He remembered the trick that Charlie Pawpaw had played on him.

The song from his dream wound through his mind. "Pickin' up pawpaws, put 'em in your pocket." Where the hell had he learned that melody?

"You got a name?" the man asked him.

"Call me Ray. What you want me to call you, honcho?"

"Harlan. Harlan Seaberry."

They looked at each other for a few seconds.

"Well?" Harlan Seaberry asked.

"Well what?"

"The horse. You want to sell it to me?"

Raider nodded. "It's yours. An' you can keep the five dollars."

"Thank you kindly!"

"But you gotta get me t' Klamath Falls," the big man added.
"Deal!"

Harlan Seaberry turned to head back down to the road.

"Seaberry?"

"Yessir?"

"Is there a wire in Klamath Falls?"

"No, not that I know of."

Raider felt his spirits sinking even lower. "Shit."

"I'm goin' to skin that horse, mister. I'll holler when I'm
ready to roll. Or you can come down and help me."

"I ain't never took much t' horse skinnin'. You do what you
have t' do an' then holler. I got stuff t' figger till then."

The man stepped down the slope, eager to reap his good fortune.

Didn't that beat all? A dead horse worth so much to a man.
Raider felt guilty for riding the pinto into the ground. The guilt
kept him from going back to sleep while Harlan Seaberry skinned
out the horse. So he pondered on his chances for catching Charlie
Pawpaw. The outlaw had half a day and a whole night head start.
The squaw was no longer with him so he could cover a lot of
ground in a hurry. That damned trick had been smart. Raider
would have to keep his eyes open for another ambush.

He stood up, brushing the dirt and leaves from his body. His
body yearned for a shot of whiskey. He searched in his saddlebags but couldn't find a bottle. So he shifted the saddle around
and sat down on it. The saddle was more comfortable than the
ground and the rain had stopped; two things to be thankful for.

Take it slow, he told himself. Stay after Pawpaw if it took
another month to catch him. Get to Klamath Falls, find a mount,
get to the nearest town that had a wire, ask Wagner for his back
pay.

"Hey, Seaberry, you through skinnin' that critter?"

"Nearabouts," the man called back.

Raider reached for his Winchester, unwrapping the oilcloth.
Best to keep it handy, in case the horse-skinner wasn't a man of
his word. But then the sky rumbled overhead and it began to rain
again, forcing him to wrap the rifle for protection. He was wet,
sore, and full of hatred for everything. Nothing to do but ride it
out and hope he could pick up Charlie Pawpaw's trail in Klamath
Falls.

● ● ●

The last thing Raider expected to find in Klamath Falls, Oregon, was a great poker game. He was having a drink at the Muddy Timber Saloon, a dark and dingy tavern where the origin of the whiskey could be debated without ever coming to any logical conclusions. A shot glass of red-eye was poised at his lips when he heard the gold coins hitting the table.

"Raise you five," a voice said.

Raider fought off the urge to turn and look at the game. Hell, he wasn't even sure he had enough money to play. A new horse would cost him most of what was in his pocket. He had also eaten a fried chicken dinner, avoiding beef since the horse-skinner had brought the pinto to town.

More coins clinked as bets were made. Music to his ears. They seemed to be playing quickly too, the sign of a good game.

Shake it off.

Things had been smoother since the big man hit Klamath Falls. True to his word, the horse-skinner had gotten him to the dismal town by nightfall. A sympathetic livery man allowed him to dry out by the fire, to oil his guns, and have a cup of coffee. He was keeping his possessions at the stable while he began his search for any sign of Charlie Pawpaw. The whiskey was just to fortify him, to chase away the chill.

"See your dollar and raise you two!"

He told himself not to turn and look. If he saw the game, he would want to play. Even though he had work to do, it was still beyond his willpower to resist a bit of fun. Hell, he hadn't been in a game for at least three months. And he— More coins clinked in the pot.

"Call!"

"Two pair. Aces over ladies."

"Three of a kind, all treys."

A silence fell over the game. Raider knew this would be the true test of the players. Sometimes a win could cause hard feelings. In a good game, hard feelings never happened.

The loser laughed. "Uhm. Thought I had that one."

Sound of a winner dragging the pile toward him. "Yep, I was wonderin' if you had the full boat buried there."

Everybody else laughed.

Raider knocked back the shot of red-eye. It burned away the skin inside his throat. No need to get involved in a game of chance, not the way his luck was running. Stay the hell away.

"Well, gents," said one of the combatants at the poker table, "I got to hang it up for the evenin'."

Good-natured protests flew around the circle. They didn't mind his leaving with his winnings so much as they didn't want to lose a player. That would reduce them to four players. They needed at least five for a good game.

Raider stiffened, knowing that he was going to surrender, but fighting it all the way. He pulled the money out of his pocket, counting it after he paid for the whiskey. Nineteen dollars and thirty cents.

"Hey, stranger?"

He really wanted to ignore the man.

"You! Big man at the bar?"

Well, he told himself, he couldn't be rude in a town where he was going to be asking a lot of questions about Charlie Pawpaw.

He turned to regard the friendly men at the card table. "You speakin' t' me, mister?"

"Need a fifth hand," the man offered. "Low stakes. Three raise limit. You interested?"

Raider licked his lips. The damned card game was the first thing that had felt right in a long time. He rationalized the diversion by telling himself that he could ask the men about the outlaw he was chasing. Maybe some of them had seen Pawpaw.

"I reckon I'm in," Raider replied.

The boys at the table whooped.

"New blood."

"Hope he's loaded."

Raider eased into a chair at the table.

"Now don't go scarin' the stranger," said a man in a gray Stetson. "He'll think we're a bunch of sharpers."

The big Pinkerton gave them his coyote grin. "Naw, I can tell a good game when I see one. You boys just deal the cards an' we'll see what happens."

The man in the gray Stetson smiled back at him. "Sounds like we got us a real poker player, boys. And he sure as hell looks lucky to me."

Suddenly Raider felt lucky. Maybe things were turning back his way. If Lady Luck slapped you in the face a hundred times, she had to kiss you at least once. His black eyes widened when the cards began to flip. He put his money on the table and prepared for battle.

"Straight to the queen," said the man with the gray Stetson.

Raider shook his head. "Full house."

All of the other players nodded appreciatively. Raider had just won his sixth straight hand. He dragged a big pile of coins and scrip across the tabletop. He kept his eyes low, trying not to enjoy his winnings too much. It wasn't polite to gloat, even when you had won almost five hundred dollars.

The Stetson man tipped back his gray hat. "Dang me if I know how you're doin' it. I know you ain't cheatin'."

"No, he ain't cheatin'," rejoined another player.

"Stayed in every hand."

"Right up till the end on every one."

Raider leaned back in his chair. "Don't worry, boys, you'll get a chance t' win some of it back. I ain't goin' nowhere. Here, let me buy a bottle for us. Barkeep, you got any real whiskey?" Maybe it was time to ask questions about Pawpaw.

The players applauded a bottle of fine Irish hooch that Raider paid twenty dollars for. He had to wonder where the men in the game got the kind of money they were losing. Best not to ask, for fear that the money might be stolen. He didn't want to know it if he was winning bad-luck money.

"Now this stranger has some breedin'. Knows the good things in life," the gray Stetson offered. "A regular gentleman."

Raider passed the cards to the man on his left. "Roll 'em."

"Five draw, no limit."

Raider nodded. "Fine by me." What would he ask first?

He could lose back a couple of hundred and grill them at the same time.

The betting got heavy, prompted by the man in the gray Stetson.

Raider figured to stay in all the way. He was dealt a pair of tens and then drew to the pair. When he spread the cards, the third ten was staring back at him. Not a great hand, but one to stick with. Ask them about Pawpaw later.

He saw every bet and raise, wondering if they could beat him.

Finally the hand was called. Stetson had to spread first. He showed them three nines.

The others backed off.

Raider put down his hand. "Three tens."

A groan from the Stetson man. "Not again."

"Well, that's it for me," said one of the players.

Two more agreed that it was time for the game to end.

Raider looked at the man with the gray Stetson. "You want to slug it out?"

"Let me think on it."

Raider dragged the pile toward him. Not a bad night. Until he heard the ruckus at the swinging doors of the Muddy Timber. The barkeeper was yelling at someone to get away.

When Raider heard the word *squaw*, he got up immediately, stuffing the money in his pockets.

"Hey, where are you goin', big man?"

"I'll be back."

Raider strode across the bar, meeting the bartender as he reentered the saloon. "What seems to be the problem, Jasper?"

A scowl from the barkeeper. "I ain't lettin' no squaw sleep in back of my house. You hear me?"

Raider nodded, agreeing that it wasn't wise to take in Indians as tenants. "You seen her afore?"

"Can't say as I— Hey, where are you goin'?"

The big Pinkerton pushed past the man, breaking through the swinging doors. He looked up one side of the street and down the other. The squaw had disappeared. He wondered if it was the same woman who had helped to trick him on the trail. If she had already turned up in Klamath Falls, then she might be looking for Pawpaw. Or they might be meeting for a prearranged rendezvous.

He started back toward the stable, wondering if it was the same woman.

The man in the gray Stetson came after him. "Hey, big man, you forgot your bottle of whiskey."

"Keep it," Raider called back. "And if I live t' see t'morrow, I'll give you a chance t' win your money back."

The man said something else, but Raider was already out of earshot. He was hoping the squaw would head for the livery. Maybe the stableman would let her sleep there in the loft.

But as he approached, he saw that the smithy was turning the woman away. Raider caught a glimpse of her before the door closed in her face. It was Pawpaw's woman all right. And Raider hoped like hell that the outlaw would come to claim his bride.

CHAPTER SIX

As soon as the squaw had cleared the entrance to the stable, Raider tore across the street and burst through the wooden door. The livery man squinted at the big Pinkerton, wondering what the hell to think about the sense of urgency on Raider's face. The man with black eyes didn't seem to be the sort who let himself get too excited about anything.

"You gotta get her t' come back," Raider said. "Hurry, afore she gets away."

The livery man frowned. "What are you talkin' about?"

"That squaw. You gotta get her t' come back. I'll explain later, just run after her afore she finds a place t' sleep."

The livery man was a short, round man with blond hair and pale eyes. He grimaced at Raider. "If you want that squaw, just go after her. But I won't have her under my roof. I've seen her before. She's trouble."

Raider didn't have time to plead his case to the proud man. "Here," he said, digging into his pockets for his poker winnings. "I'll give you twenty dollars if you'll run after her an' bring her back. Don't tell her I'm here. An' hang a lantern high up, there, so there'll be light over the door an' I can see."

"Nobody's gonna tell me how to run my own business!"

Raider couldn't blame him. "Fifty dollars. In gold an' silver."

The man's pale eyes widened. "If you want her that bad, then you ought to be able to sweeten the pot."

Raider called his bluff. "Forget it, I'll find somebody else t'—"

"Fifty is fine."

The money changed hands.

"What do you want me to do with her when I get her back here?" the livery man asked as he lit the lantern to hang over the door.

Raider waved him toward the street. "Just make her sleep downstairs. Don't let her come into the loft. An' don't get in the way if a man shows up to ask about her. Yeah, that lantern does the trick. I'll be able t' see fine."

"You a lawman?"

"No, but I'm gonna take that money back if you don't go out an' do what I paid you for."

Without another word, the stable man was off after the squaw.

Raider climbed into the loft, drawing back into the shadows. He checked his guns, which he had oiled earlier while he was drying out in front of the smithy's fire. He checked the load on the Winchester and then fingered the cylinder of his Colt. Five full chambers. He slipped a cartridge into the sixth empty chamber. If Charlie Pawpaw showed up to look for the woman, Raider had to be ready. No more pussyfooting. Even if it meant killing the man who had robbed Wells Fargo.

Raider tensed when he heard the door swing open downstairs. The livery man came in, leading the squaw's horse. Raider realized he should have taken it from her when he caught her in the woods. He might have been able to catch Pawpaw if he had brought the extra mount with him. He told himself to stop second-guessing and concentrate on the matters at hand.

Noises drifted up from the stable as the livery man bedded down the squaw's horse. After he had finished with the animal, he proceeded to bed down the squaw, who didn't protest very much. They grunted and groaned for a while, probably less than ten minutes, although it seemed like an eternity to the aching man in the loft.

When the livery man had finished his business, he got up and retired for the night. Raider leaned back against the wall, listening as the squaw began to snore. What if Pawpaw wasn't going to come back after her? After all, he should have gotten to Klamath Falls before her. Unless he had taken another route. Or maybe he had to walk his mule because it now carried the remainder of his stolen fortune.

Raider considered climbing down the ladder and making her talk. He wondered what tribe she was from. Some Indians were just so tough that nothing could get them to open their mouths. She was probably from a northwestern tribe, Spokane maybe. What the hell was she to Charlie Pawpaw?

He leaned forward when he heard the door open again downstairs. Maybe this was it. He listened closely, only to hear the livery man coming back for a second round with the squaw. She didn't seem to mind being awakened. Raider vowed that he would find a soft, sweet-smelling woman as soon as he had Pawpaw in custody. The livery man finally got up and left again.

The squaw resumed her snoring.

Raider tried to close his eyes but he was too nervous. He didn't want any kind of carelessness to get in the way if the outlaw showed his face. So he sat there, staying awake most of the night. When he finally did doze off, he had the dream about the dying pinto. His head snapped up and he listened to the rain that beat down on the roof of the stable.

Another storm. That might keep Pawpaw away from his woman. Or maybe she was just running away on her own. Maybe he didn't give a damn about her at all, would've killed her if she hadn't been of some use to him.

That damned trick had really gotten Raider's goat.

He leaned back, trying not to close his eyes.

But his mind drifted away and pretty soon he was back on the pinto again, reliving its untimely death.

In his dream, he heard the pinto speaking, only it wasn't the horse. A voice rattled him awake. It rose from below, along with the squeaking of the stable door. His eyes opened to the pale gray glow of predawn.

A man's voice called into the stable. "Little Duck?"

Raider reached for his Colt. He would need the pistol in close quarters. Best to get it over with quickly. Get the drop, give the outlaw one chance to surrender, then put a bullet between his eyes.

"Little Duck? It's me, Charlie."

Raider eased to the edge of the loft and peered down at the

short, ugly outlaw. He thumbed the hammer of the revolver, taking careful aim. He started to say something but the Indian woman ran to throw her arms around Charlie Pawpaw. Raider realized then that the outlaw and his squaw had heard the clicking of the Colt's loaded cylinder.

Sometimes things happen too fast, like a herd of cattle stampeding over you. You never expect to be out of control. But reflexes have a way of taking over when a gun starts barking in your face. The only thing that matters then is saving your own life.

Raider heard the Indian woman shout, "It's the Pinkerton!"

Charlie Pawpaw reached for his sidearm.

Raider told him to hold it but the outlaw didn't listen. A Remington exploded, sending lead into the boards of the loft. Pawpaw had aimed too low with his first two shots.

The squaw was standing in front of Pawpaw. Raider could only see the outlaw's head and the flash of the Remington's muzzle. He was already locked in on him. Slow squeeze of the trigger. One shot erupted from the barrel of the Colt.

Charlie Pawpaw screamed. He fell against the squaw and then onto the floor of the livery. Blood ran from his right eye where Raider's bullet had entered. The slug had come out the back, taking half of the outlaw's skull with it.

Raider held steady as the smoke cleared. He wanted to see what the squaw was going to do. She had bent over the twitching corpse of her dying lover.

"He ain't gonna make it, honey. He—"

She cried out, grabbing the gun from Pawpaw's warm hand. Raider knew she was going to shoot, but he didn't want to kill her. It was bad luck to kill a woman, even if she was taking aim.

He aimed carefully, warning her, hoping to wing her gun hand if she didn't let up. She didn't let up. He squeezed the Colt's trigger again, only to watch the squaw step into the line of the bullet. She buckled when the slug tore through her heart. The Remington went off but the slug was nowhere near Raider when it landed.

Smoke swirled up toward him. He sat still, waiting to see if both of them were really finished. He raised the Colt again when the livery man rushed in to see what had happened.

"It's only me, cowboy!"

He lowered the barrel of his gun. "You coulda got yourself shot by runnin' in like that."

The livery man's eyes widened. "Dang. What the devil happened?"

Raider holstered up and climbed down the ladder. He tipped back his Stetson, gazing down at the bodies. "That one's an outlaw named Pawpaw. She's his squaw. I was hopin' he'd show t' look for her."

His stomach was churning. No matter how many times he killed a man, he always had that aching in his belly afterward. It would fade away eventually.

"What'd he do?" the livery man asked.

Raider sighed. "He stole a bunch o' money. Which means he's prob'ly got a couple o' horses runnin' 'round outside. You stay here while I have a look-see. An' don't touch neither one of 'em."

"You gonna leave me here alone?"

"I won't be long."

The look in the stableman's eyes told Raider that he would not be rifling the corpses for their loot. Raider knew he would have to search both of them after he found Pawpaw's horses.

The gunshots had spooked Pawpaw's mule, chasing it into the morning shadows. Raider found it drinking at a water trough. It was loaded down like a prospector's burro. Maybe Pawpaw had been carrying all the stolen money with him. Raider led the mule back to the stable.

"I didn't touch 'em," said the livery man. "And they sure as sin didn't move neither."

Raider nodded toward Pawpaw's bulk. "Do me a favor, smithy. Go through his pockets."

The man frowned. "What?"

"I gotta see everythin' he's carryin'."

"Why you want *me* to do it?"

"You can keep half of what you find on him," the big man offered.

"Where you want me to start?"

"Just do it."

As the stableman began to search the body of Charlie Pawpaw, Raider turned to the load on the back of the mule. The animal was lathered and tired. That was how the squaw had been able to beat Pawpaw to Klamath Falls. The plan had been for her to lead Raider away and then meet later in town. Pawpaw had walked all the way. Raider wondered why he hadn't passed him on the trail.

"Look here," the man said behind him. "Thirty dollars. That means fifteen of it's mine."

Raider glanced over his shoulder. "Nothin' else?"

"Like what?"

"Oh, I don' know, like a map or somethin'. Like mebbe he hid somethin' an' then made a chart so he could get back to it."

"Nothin' like that."

"Keep lookin'."

He started to unload the mule. The bulk of the money was hidden inside a bedroll. The clumps of scrip were placed carefully side by side in thin piles. Raider counted eight thousand out of the original ten that had been stolen by the outlaw. That left about two thousand somewhere else.

Raider went through the belongings again, searching until he found the canteen that felt too heavy. He asked the smith to break it open with one of his hammers. He told him to be careful.

Using a chisel, the smith managed to cut open the canteen, revealing the disk-shaped hunk of gold inside.

"Glory be," said the stableman.

"He melted down the coins," Raider offered. "Poured all the gold into the canteen."

"Don't take much to melt gold."

Raider glanced at the man's wide eyes. "Don't get no ideas, pardner. Not less'n you wanna end up like them two there."

"I never did find nothin' else on him." He looked at the gold again and then at the pile of paper money. "Damn. He's got all this on him, but he's carryin' thirty dollars in his pockets."

Raider shrugged. "Makes sense. Anybody who'd waylay him would be happy t' find thirty dollars. He could give it up without a fight, claim it was his life savin's, beg somebody not t' rob him. Meantime, he's got the mother lode rolled up in his blanket an' his canteen. An' it looks like it's all here."

The man whistled. "I don't reckon you'd split it with me."

Raider shook his head. "Sorry, pardner. I gotta take it back t' the Wells Fargo people. You wouldn't know where the nearest wire is, would you?"

"Medford. There's a Wells Fargo office there too."

That was what the big man wanted to hear. If he took the

money back, nobody would be worried about the body of Charlie Pawpaw. Raider wasn't crazy about the idea of traveling with all that loot on him, but he had to make sure it got back into the right hands. It was what he had been hired to do.

"You got any law in this town?" he asked.

"Justice of the peace, but he don't like to be woke up for trouble. Lives out on the edge of town, near the lake. You want me to ride out and get him?"

"No." He looked at the bodies. "There's no need for that. It might be a good idea t' keep this 'tween you an' me."

The smithy nodded. "I'm happy. I got thirty bucks out of this."

"Fifteen," Raider reminded him. "You and me was gonna split that."

The man frowned. "Aw, I helped you, didn't I?"

"You didn't face no gunfire, boy. An' I gave you a wad o' cash t' bring that squaw back here."

"Well, can I at least keep the mule?"

Raider exhaled defeatedly. "No. Keep the thirty. I gotta use that mule t' haul the body north."

The livery man rubbed his chin. "Got to take the body, huh."

Raider thought he saw an opening. "You got an undertaker in this town?"

"No, not really."

"What about a cemetery?"

A frown on the man's rugged face. "A what?"

"A graveyard."

"I can't never remember nobody dyin' around here since I been in town. But I reckon there's a graveyard here."

Raider nodded appreciatively. "Aw right, pardner, this is it. I wanna leave here t'night an' you want the mule."

"So?"

"Just this," the big man continued, "those bodies gotta be put in the ground t'morrow mornin'—"

"I ain't gonna dig no grave!"

"No, that ain't it. I just want you t' wait till the justice wakes up an' then go tell him what happened. I can write it down for you if you want me to. Or the justice can check with my boss."

The man frowned, shaking his head. "I don't know. He ain't really a lawman. Don't carry no gun. Course, he might need some kind of license to bury them."

Raider knew what that meant. A bribe. The livery man wanted money in case he had to grease the justice's palm. And if the justice went along with the story, then the smithy kept the extra cash.

"How much?" Raider asked.

He still had the poker money on him. It would be easier to pay than to drag the body back to Medford. Besides, a corpse attracted a lot of attention and a man with ten thousand dollars didn't want that.

"Fifty more oughta do it," the smith said.

Raider dug into his pocket, pulling out the wad of cash. "Here's a hundred more. An' I get the pick o' the mounts in your stable."

"Any horse but the gray—"

"I want the gray." He held out the money. "Take it or leave it, bud. If I wait for the justice, you'll lose it all."

He didn't have to think about it for very long. "Okay. And you write it down so I got somethin' to show the justice."

Raider agreed, although he hated to write. It would be like doing a report for Wagner. Hell, everything would be all right. The good town of Klamath Falls could bury Pawpaw and his woman. Raider just wanted to get the hell away, to put that money in the place where it rightfully belonged. Charlie Pawpaw wasn't going anywhere. If somebody wanted to find him later, the smith could always direct them to the outlaw's grave. The money was the important thing.

When he finished writing his statement for the stableman, he put the money in his saddlebags. "Don't get any ideas 'bout followin' me," he warned as he saddled the gray.

"I won't, mister. I sure as hell won't."

He watched as Raider swung into the saddle and rode west, away from Klamath Falls. He had already decided to bury the corpses up by the lake. Nobody would ever know. And there sure as hell wasn't any need to tell the justice about the shootings. It would only cause trouble, especially if he had to give up some of the Pinkerton's money.

CHAPTER SEVEN

The machinations of the journey had been interminable for William Wagner, though, in fact, he had been making good time all the way.

Three quick trains had put him in Omaha in four days. There he was able to enlist a lawyer for counsel in Lincoln. The attorney was agreeable to traveling, so Wagner had immediately hired a carriage to take them the rest of the way. Lincoln could be reached in less than a day by coach, or at least that was what the driver told him.

The bumpy ride was hellish for Wagner. His biggest fear was for the man who awaited trial in Lincoln. Avery had only done his duty. There was no reason to punish him for it.

But when they reached Lincoln in the wee hours of the morning, Wagner was informed by the jailer that Avery's trial had been moved to a place called Milford, west of Lincoln, where the trouble had happened. The Milford sheriff had come with the papers.

The lawyer took Wagner aside. "It's a railroad job. This is the capital. There's more than one judge here. Your man could have been tried in Lincoln."

Wagner turned to the jailer. "When is Avery supposed to be tried?"

"Tomorrow. At ten o'clock."

"I don't like it," the attorney said. "We've got to reach him if we're going to have a chance."

Wagner stormed out of the jail with the counselor behind him. "How long will it take you to get to Milford?" he called to the driver.

The man shrugged. "I'll need new horses."

"I don't care what it takes, as long as you can get us there by ten o'clock tomorrow morning."

"Done!" the driver replied.

And true to the man's word, the coach rolled into Milford, Nebraska, at ten minutes after ten.

Wagner saw the crowd gathered in front of the saloon, where the trial was taking place. Spectators jockeyed for position, trying to get a glimpse of the Pinkerton who was on trial. Most of them hoped to stay for a hanging afterward.

"Let's hurry," he called to the barrister.

They pushed their way into the saloon, moving down the middle aisle toward the defendant, P. W. Avery, who sat alone at a table. His hands were in chains. He sat up straight and smiled when he saw Wagner.

An old judge stared down his nose at the two interlopers whose surprise appearance had brought drama to the crowd.

"Order!" cried the gray-haired magistrate. "Order in this court."

Avery tried to stand up but the sheriff pushed down on his shoulders. "Stay still, Avery." He pointed at Wagner. "And you can get the hell out of here, mister."

The lawyer stepped in front of Wagner. "Your honor, Mr. Avery has right to legal counsel. Has he been provided with an attorney?"

The judge squinted and glared at the sheriff. "Well? Has he?"

"He don't need no book-thumpin' weasel," the sheriff cried. "Let's get on with this trial."

"Objection!" the lawyer cried. "I'd like to move that this trial be postponed until I have had a chance to confer with my client."

The sheriff started to complain, but the judge rapped his gavel. "Motion is granted. I'll be back through here in two weeks to take this matter to trial if it hasn't been settled by then."

"But judge!"

He pointed the gavel at the lawman. "Now look here, Simpson, this man has a right to a lawyer, just like this young man said." He smiled at the attorney. "Where did you study law, boy?"

"On my own, sir. And I was helped by a friend of my family."

"Commendable. You have two weeks to prepare your case."

Everyone was disappointed, with the exception of Wagner, Avery, and the attorney. The sheriff grabbed Avery's shoulder, insisting that he stay in custody. The attorney moved for Avery's release on bail. Bail was denied, as Avery was charged with murder.

"Score one for the sheriff," Wagner said as Avery was led away in chains.

The attorney sighed. "We're not through this yet."

Wagner frowned. "The judge seemed agreeable."

The lawyer shook his head. "No. He just wants to go fishing. I know him. Judge Tinnley. He's one of these folks, grew up in Lincoln, spent his whole life in these parts. Of course, I'd rather try the case before him instead of taking it to a jury. He might listen to the facts, at least."

Wagner nodded, patting him on the shoulder. "Go see Avery. Get what information you can from him. I'll meet you at the carriage later. We'll have to find accommodations. And I have a lot of messages to send north. I'm pretty sure Mr. Pinkerton will want me to stay here until this is settled."

When Allan Pinkerton received Wagner's wire, he turned to one of his clerks and told him to take down a message. "Tell William that he's to stay in Nebraska until Avery is set free. Keep me notified on the trial. And wire him another two hundred dollars."

"Yes, sir."

Pinkerton turned back into his office. Wagner seemed to have the Avery situation under control. It worked out better. He didn't want to send Raider into the fray. He had another assignment for the big man from Arkansas. And as soon as he heard from the rough-and-tumble gunslinger, he was going to get him started on his next assignment.

CHAPTER EIGHT

Ten days after he had killed Charlie Pawpaw and the squaw, Raider was in Medford, Oregon, waiting for a reply from the home office. The wire had gone down somewhere along the way. He was able to get his message out, but nothing had come in for a couple of days.

Everything else had worked out to Raider's satisfaction. He made it through the wooded trails without mishap, arriving in the pretty little town with the money still in his possession. A couple of times he had met strangers along the way, but nobody had threatened him. Who would've bothered to mess with such a dangerous, scraggly-looking rider? Only the toughest guns had enough guts to cross a tall, black-eyed stranger with a Colt hanging so low on his hip.

The man at the Wells Fargo office had grimaced when the rough-hewn agent filled the doorway. He half expected a robbery, at least until Raider introduced himself and produced his credentials. The Wells Fargo man said that Raider didn't look like any Pinkerton that he had ever seen.

"I was hired t' catch Charlie Pawpaw," the big man had said.

The clerk's eyes had bugged out. "What happened?"

"I caught him."

Raider had dropped the money on the counter. "Ten thousand. Or at least close to it. Eight in paper, the rest in gold."

At first Raider had figured there might be a problem, but as luck would have it, the man who had hired him worked in Medford. He was summoned from the back room by the clerk. He was damned surprised to see Raider.

"Back so soon?"

"You wanna count it an' sign a paper sayin' I brought it t' you?" Raider had asked.

The Wells Fargo agent couldn't count fast enough. He was as happy as a kid with a new toy. Raider felt sort of good about returning the money, but he couldn't really get excited about it. The case was over. Time to take a rest and get on to other business.

No one questioned the whereabouts of Charlie Pawpaw. Raider merely said that Pawpaw was dead and buried. The big man still felt guilty about having to kill the squaw. He wondered how much bad luck it would bring, although things finally seemed to be turning his way.

Until the wire went down.

The rest was doing him some good. He took a room in the best boarding house he could find. His winnings from the poker game in Klamath Falls had come in handy. Good food, new clothes, a warm bed. He was having trouble finding a woman though. The town whore had gone up to Portland to visit with her sister, so pickings had been slim. There wasn't even a decent place to get a drink.

The lone saloon of Medford was in back of a general store. The owner had set up a couple of chairs and a few tables. Raider only went in there once to buy a bottle. The storekeeper had made him pay twenty dollars for it. Raider had been resentful of the steep price, until he realized that the whiskey would be his only diversion in Medford.

During his third day in Medford, the telegraph key began working again. Raider sent another wire to the home office, to make sure his message got through. "Settled with Wells Fargo. Ready to ride." Short and to the point. He had written another report that was posted from Medford, but the wire would get there long before the letter did.

There was nothing to do but wait. Lying on his bed in the boarding house, he wished he could ride back to Klamath Falls and find the gamblers. They had been good players. And Raider figured they deserved a chance to get their money back. Why the hell did Medford have to be so straitlaced? A man needed recreation in the company of willing women. But the ladies of Medford looked away when he tipped his new Stetson to them. He couldn't blame them. Proper women wanted a man to put rings on their fingers and then they wanted to put one through *his* nose. Raider had a less permanent arrangement in mind. But it didn't seem like it was going to happen.

When he dozed off, he had dreams about San Francisco. The dream about the Chinese girl always haunted him when he had been too long between women. He saw Madam Wu in the dream. He remembered her little shows, the way the lights had flickered on the walls. The Chinese girl had tried to get him to smoke opium, but the big man always refrained.

When he opened his eyes, he felt sort of sad about Madam Wu. She had been killed by the Tong, a secret Chinese society. Raider wondered if the old girl's operation was still around. The establishment had featured gaming tables for blackjack and poker, Raider's favorite games of chance. He sat on the edge of the bed, wishing he was anywhere but Oregon.

What the hell time was it? Dark outside. He leaned back again but he wasn't sleepy. Thoughts of San Francisco haunted him again. He never longed for a city, but he knew that 'Frisco was a place where a man could find the things that kept his spirit alive. Raider had to admit the city by the bay held some fascination for him. His visits there had never been dull.

Raider considered leaving the boarding house, waking the livery man and riding south on the gray. He could send a wire to Wagner, advising him of his movements. Hit San Francisco in a couple of weeks, a week and a half if he traveled nights. No, he'd give the gray a break. He knew it wasn't right to ride a horse into the ground the way he had done the pinto. It was a stupid damned move any way you looked at it. He decided to stay in Medford until word came from Wagner.

A cock crowed outside his window. Sunup soon. The telegraph office didn't open till eight. So he closed his eyes and finally drifted off again, dreaming of San Francisco. He was languishing at Madam Wu's when the knocking woke him from his reverie. Somebody was at his door.

He reached for the Colt, which was hanging on the bedpost. "Who is it?"

"Me, from the telegraph office," a voice cried. "You got a telegram first thing this mornin'. I thought I'd bring it over to you. You got some money, too."

Raider dressed and let the man in. "What's it say?"

The key operator frowned. "Well, says you're supposed to go to San Francisco as soon as you get this."

Raider smiled. "Don't look so hangdog, friend, that's good news. What time is it?"

"Ten o'clock."

Raider pushed back a curtain to let in the morning sun. Not a cloud in the sky. He had to feel good about his recent lucky streak.

"Got some money here," the operator said. "Back pay. Seventy-six dollars. Sixty in gold, the rest in paper."

"Keep a dollar for your trouble," Raider said as he took the money from him. "Go on, you earned it."

The man smiled. "Thanks. I mean, I wasn't expectin' nothin'. I just wanted you to get the message."

"I got it. You can go now."

"Don't you want to hear the rest?"

Raider nodded, "Okay. Let's have it."

"You're supposed to see a man name of John Sanders. Meet him on the twenty-fifth at the Grandview Hotel. Ask for him at the front desk."

Raider's brow fretted. "What day is it?"

"Thursday."

"I mean the date."

"The twelfth," replied the operator.

Raider laughed a little. "Too good t' be true. I should be able t' make it with no trouble."

"You gonna ride?" the operator asked.

Raider gestured to the door. "I reckon that's my bus'ness, boy. Now you go on an' tend yours."

"Sure. Thanks for the buck, mister."

Raider gathered his belongings and started for the livery. He could have waited for the boarding house's big lunch, but he decided to pick up some supplies at the general store. No need to hang around Medford, not with San Francisco on the horizon.

He wanted a smooth ride through the hills and valleys of northern California. He had decided to stay away from trouble. And he managed to avoid all complications on the trail, at least until he stopped in Yreka, California, to have a drink.

Raider had never been in the cantina that sat on the southern boundary of Yreka. When he rode up on the dusty mud and straw bodega, he saw no sign to announce the presence of liquor for sale. But the place had a look about it, a few horses tied in front, smoke from a mud chimney. The sun was pretty much gone to the west, leaving a dull orange glow behind it.

The big man from Arkansas tied the gray at the hitching post. He patted the strong animal on the neck. Four days on the trail without a hitch. He'd let the gray drink when it had cooled off.

Everybody turned to look at the tall man who entered the dim room. A low fire and a couple of candles were the only light. Raider didn't hesitate as he strode toward the rough counter that served as a bar.

The cantina man nodded to him. "Yeah?"

"You got anything that you didn't make yourself?"

"No."

Raider shrugged. "Then give me the best of what you got to offer."

The man served him a warm drink that burned a little going down. Strong, brown liquid distilled from God knew where. It hit Raider's stomach and set it on fire.

"Any food?"

"Stew."

Raider motioned for him to refill his wooden mug. He told the man to bring him a bowl of the stew. It was probably horse meat— if he was lucky.

The stew wasn't that bad and the man served bread with it.

Raider was sopping the bowl with the last piece of bread when he felt a hand on his shoulder. He turned quickly, drawing his Colt. He put the barrel under the man's chin.

"Hey, big 'un, it's only me. Or don't you play poker with the same man twice in a row?"

Raider recognized the man with the gray Stetson from Klamath Falls. "Pardner, I reckon it's about time you told me your name."

"Call me Trueluck."

Raider nodded.

Trueluck motioned him toward the table across the room. "Come on, I got a bottle of the real thing."

Raider didn't have to be coaxed. He offered his mug, which was filled with smooth, Kentucky whiskey. The glow of the bourbon fended off the sick feeling of the homebrew. Raider felt no pain in his tired body.

"Where you headin', Ray?" Trueluck asked.

Raider eyed the man. He was still clad in the same neat gray suit that matched his Stetson. Grayish hair. Lined face. He didn't look like a gambler, not a professional anyway.

"You followin' me, Trueluck?"

A shrug from the man in the Stetson. "No. I'm headin' down Stockton way. Hopin' to buy some cattle."

Raider thought that was a good enough explanation, at least for the time being. "Sorry I ran out on you in Klamath Falls. I had some business come up, took me outta town pretty quick."

Trueluck nodded. "Ain't no never mind to me. Man has a right to take what he's won fair and square. We couldn't keep you there all night. The game was about over anyway."

Raider grimaced. "You were the big loser."

Trueluck waved him off. "If you can't stand to lose once in a while, then you don't deserve to win."

"Makes sense t' me."

Raider drank the whiskey, listening to Trueluck as he went on about the cattle business. Seems a man could make money these days by buying a bunch of cows in one place and selling them in another for more money. And it was a hell of a lot better than raising the damned things yourself. Trueluck hated cows when he thought about it, but he sure as hell liked making money on them.

He took out a deck of cards and started to shuffle them.

"Think we can get a game goin'?" Raider asked.

Trueluck said to wait and see. The only other inhabitants of the cantina were too drunk and too poor to play cards. If anybody else showed up, a game was a possibility. But Trueluck really didn't like the look of the cantina. Like Raider, he had merely stopped to wet his whistle.

Raider suggested showdown for a dollar a hand. Trueluck nodded and started to roll the cards. Five cards up for him, five up for Raider. Best hand takes the dollar. Raider won the first one and then lost eight in a row.

"Too rich for you?" Trueluck asked with a smile.

Raider shrugged. "Keep dealin'. I got enough dollars t' stay with you for a while. Course, us workin' men run outta money sooner or later."

Raider won five straight and then lost nine more.

Trueluck grimaced. "Hell, this is borin', even if I am winnin'."

Raider was going to suggest that they up the stakes, but before he could offer the suggestion, three men pushed into the murky cantina. They were young and loud. Not the kind to ask to play poker.

Trueluck put his cards away. He was staring at the tallest of the three men, a blond rider with a sombrero strung on his back.

"Tequila!" the blond man said.

Raider looked at Trueluck. "You know him?"

"He's called Johnny Sonora. Ever heard of him?"

Raider shook his head. "Can't say as I have."

"Ever hear of the California Kid?"

Raider frowned. "Yeah, I killed him a couple o' years back."

"Must've been another California Kid," Trueluck offered.

"You look like you're afraid of him," Raider challenged. "Hell, he prob'ly ain't more'n any other punk kid with a gun."

As he said it, Johnny Sonora turned toward Raider, looking straight at him as if he had heard what Raider had said. But when he locked eyes with the black-eyed stranger, Sonora immediately turned away. Raider didn't think much of it, even when the three men began to argue.

It started small at first. A disagreement that was laughed off. Then came the second disagreement, which escalated into shouting.

Trueluck started to get up.

Raider stopped him. "Just stay low if they start shootin'. You won't make it out if you go now."

Raider was right. Johnny Sonora backed away from his two friends, glaring at them. His hand was hanging low over a brand-new, ivory-handled Peacemaker.

"You want it all, Sonora!"

The California Kid smiled an eerie grin. Cold, calculating, like he had meant for this to happen. He wanted to kill the two men. Who could say he was not in the right? Hell, he was facing two guns.

"I got a right," Sonora said. "Go on, pull if you're—"

They both pulled.

Raider pushed Trueluck to the floor.

Johnny Sonora's hand was moving. Raider couldn't believe how fast the kid drew and killed both of his companions. Raider's own Colt was up, but he had to wonder if the kid had been quicker.

"You all saw it!" cried Johnny Sonora. "They drew first!"

He turned to regard Raider, who held his Colt steady. "Ain't got no truck with you, big man."

Raider waved the Colt toward the door. "They drew first, boy. Now you vamoose. Go on."

Sonora pointed a finger at the big man. "I'll see you again."

"Not if I see you first."

The California Kid darted into the night, galloping away from the cantina as fast as his mount would take him.

Trueluck looked up from the floor. "Is it finished?"

Raider nodded, holstering his Colt. "Yeah an' so am I."

"Where you goin'?" Trueluck asked.

Raider had started for the door. "South."

"Can I ride with you?"

"No."

Raider didn't want any traveling companions. Look what had happened to Johnny Sonora's friends. Raider just wanted to ride alone and get the hell to San Francisco while he was still alive.

CHAPTER NINE

Raider reached San Francisco fifteen days after he had left Oregon. It bothered him that he was a day late. He was supposed to meet the man named John Sanders on the twenty-fifth and here Raider was, riding in on the twenty-sixth. He had not pushed the gray because he still felt guilty about the last horse he had run into the ground. There was nothing he could do about it now. Just ride through the streets of 'Frisco, looking for the Grandview Hotel. He wondered if Sanders was the kind to be angry about things like tardiness. He might send word back to the agency, putting Raider in hot tar with Pinkerton and Wagner. The big man always felt like his bosses would fire him someday, if they ever stopped needing his violent services. Hell, he couldn't be a Pinkerton forever—unless a bullet cut him down before retirement.

Raider shivered. San Francisco was always as cold as Montana. And the people stared at him as he rode down the center of the street. That was how he could tell they were civilized. Citified folks always gaped at a dangerous-looking tall man in the saddle. Raider was a threat to them and their newfangled way of life. He pulled his slicker over the Colt and covered the butt of his Winchester on the sling ring of his saddle. No need to scare the women and children on the sidewalk.

53

He had forgotten how cities smelled; like a dead polecat that had been ripening for a few days in the sun. Only you could ride away from the polecat. The city smell hung in the streets and back alleys, permeating the air where no one could ride away from it.

Still, a man had to endure certain indignities if he wanted to have some of the finer things in life. Raider hoped he would have time to visit the waterfront before he went off into service for John Sanders—if he took the case. Sanders might not even want him on the case, not with him being so late. It couldn't have been avoided. If Sanders didn't want Raider, he could wire the home office for somebody else. Raider wouldn't mind a bit.

Raider had little trouble finding the Grandview Hotel. It looked to be too rich for his blood, what with the fancy columns and the doorman in a gray monkey suit. Best to get his business over with and seek shelter in a hotel that still catered to cowboys —if there was such a thing in San Francisco.

The doorman stopped him as he approached the entrance. "Hey, there, hombre," the man said, condescending. "You lose your dogie?"

Raider glared at the doorman. "Got business in this fancy barn here, Jasper. You wanna hold my horse while I take care of it?"

The doorman glared up at the tall, black-eyed ruffian. "Look here, cowboy, you ain't got no business here. Why don't you ride off down to Merchant Street, there's fleabags galore down there."

Raider wondered if he was going to have a scuffle before he even got into the place. "I'm s'posed t' meet a man name o' Sanders, he's—"

The doorman immediately took the reins from him. "Why didn't you say so? You're the Pinkerton, right?"

Raider nodded. "Yeah, how'd—"

"We've been expectin' you, cowboy. I'll take care of this nag for you. Just go in and see the man at the front desk."

Raider insisted on taking his rifle and his saddlebags before the man led the gray to the livery. "Well," he said to himself, "Sanders knows I'm late. Might as well face the music."

The lobby was the fanciest place that Raider had ever seen. He ignored the finely dressed citizens who gaped at him as he strode toward the front desk. The clerk was as surprised to see him as the doorman had been.

"Sir, don't put those saddlebags there. And please, cover up that rifle. Who the devil do you think you are, anyway?"

"I'm the man lookin' for John Sanders," Raider replied.

"Oh." He hit a bell on the front desk, summoning a bellhop. "Take this gentleman's things to room three-fourteen. And you may sign the register here, sir."

Raider grimaced at the clerk. "I ain't stayin' in this palace," the big man replied. "I'll clear out soon's I see Sanders."

"But Mr. Sanders has not yet arrived," the clerk offered. "He's been unavoidably detained. And he's instructed me to make sure that you have every comfort available to you while you wait."

Raider smiled a little. "Any o' that comfort come in a dress or a nightgown, Jasper?"

The clerk blushed. "I beg your pardon!"

"Yeah, I reckon you would." He waved off the bellhop and turned to the clerk again. "I can't afford this place, honcho. I'll go wait somewhere else till Sanders shows up."

"You don't understand," the clerk replied. "Mr. Sanders is paying for everything. There will be no charge to you personally."

Raider hesitated, but then when he considered it more closely he realized it would be bad manners to refuse Sanders's hospitality. "Okay," he started, "let me see what I need."

"You have only to name it," the clerk insisted. "Within reason, of course."

"How 'bout a reasonable bath?"

"Done."

"A reasonable barber."

The clerk nodded.

Raider figured if Sanders was such a rich gentleman, then he should see him at his best. "Some new clothes, biggest size you can find."

A frown from the clerk. "Well—"

"I'll pay. An' give whoever fetches 'em a dollar for his trouble."

"I'll go!" the bellhop chimed in.

Raider had to recognize the respect given to a dollar, even in a big place like San Francisco. It seemed to him that people spent entirely too much time worrying about money. Raider rarely gave it a second thought and he always seemed to have more than he needed.

"Food," he went on, "the biggest steak you can find with some onions an' potatoes. A pot o' black coffee."

"I shall see to it at once."

"An' whiskey, the best Irish whiskey you can find. An' if you can't find Irish, make it Canadian an' then Kentuckian. You got all that?"

The clerk nodded. "There's a bathtub in your room, sir. I'll have everything else sent up."

Raider reached into his pocket, palming a five-dollar gold piece. He was still flush with back pay and gambling winnings. Spread a little of it around. He didn't believe in making anyone work for free.

"An' I want you t' go check on my horse," Raider told the clerk. "Make sure he's all right."

"Me? I have better things to—"

Raider lifted the gold coin into the clerk's line of vision.

"But then again, we were told to make you happy, sir."

He took the coin and put it in his coat pocket. "What kind of horse is it?"

"A gray. An' make sure they shine my saddle."

"Yes, sir."

Raider snapped his fingers and the bellhop picked up his gear. Funny, he thought, how a man would sacrifice all his dignity and pride for the shiny glint of a dollar. It didn't seem right, somehow, but that was the way things seemed to go in the world.

The man carried his bags to the third floor, puffing all the way.

So this was what it was like to be rich, Raider thought. Have everybody else do your work for you. Hell, if he was rich, he could hire another Pinkerton to solve his cases for him.

"Here we are. Three-fourteen."

He opened the door for Raider.

The big man stepped into a room that was fancier than any cathouse he had ever been in. Everything was fluffy and white, lace on the curtains and pillows. More suited to a woman than a man.

"You like it?" the bellhop asked.

Raider frowned a little. "No. You got any rooms that ain't so—so ladylike?"

"This is the second best room in the place!" the bellhop offered.

"Who's got the best room?"

"Mr. Sanders, when he gets here."

Raider exhaled, thinking that it was a pain to be rich. You had to act all proper and such. Of course, it was sort of fun to have people stepping for you. He handed the bellhop two paper dollars.

"Gee, thanks!"

"Now run on an' get me them clothes. Remember, the biggest sizes you can find. Get jeans an' a shirt like I got on. An' then get a fancy shirt, a pair of black pants, an' a string tie."

The bellhop pointed to his Stetson. "Take that hat?"

"Okay. Here. An' help me pull off these boots."

He sat down in a fine chair, leaning back as the bellhop relieved him of his boots. "Take 'em and have 'em shined."

"Yes, sir. Anything else?"

Raider couldn't think of a thing.

The bellhop left in a hurry.

Raider wondered if this was the way kings acted when they dealt with their subjects. The big man from Arkansas didn't feel like much of a king. He was already growing bored with the trappings of wealth. Not much to it, he thought. Best to enjoy it while it was there and then get on with business when Sanders finally showed up. At least he wasn't really late now.

He decided to look for the bathtub.

Raider leaned back in the chair, lifting the shot glass to his lips. The Canadian whiskey went down as smoothly as water. His belly was full of good beef, his body covered with new clothes. His Stetson had been cleaned and blocked, his boots shined and stitched by a good cobbler. He had only been in San Francisco for a couple of hours, but he already felt like a different man.

Sanders still hadn't arrived, but that didn't matter. As long as his new employer took care of everything, Raider figured to enjoy himself. Sanders could show when he was damned well ready.

The big man was almost satisfied. He glanced toward the bed. A good sleep was in order, only he didn't feel sleepy. Instead, he was remorseful that the bed was empty. Such a fancy bed should have a woman in it.

The damned desk clerk hadn't been much help. Of course, there was always the waterfront. It had been dark for about an hour. If he walked all the way, he could make it in time for the evening's activities. He wondered about the day of the week. Friday or Saturday night would be best for his kind of fun, although it wasn't impossible to find action on a weeknight, especially in San Francisco.

He was getting up to look for a calendar when someone knocked on the door.

Raider hesitated, wondering if he should grab his Colt. "Who is it?"

"My name is Dennison, sir. I've come to assist you."

Raider opened the door, glaring at the man who was dressed in a black suit. "I ain't in need of no more assistance, friend. Tell the clerk that he can—"

Dennison smiled at him, affecting the graces of a well-mannered groom. "You don't understand, sir. Mr. Sanders sent me. He's been delayed in Sacramento and won't be here until tomorrow morning."

Raider gestured toward the elegant chamber. "Well, I reckon I oughta thank you for all this. You work for Sanders?"

"I'm his personal assistant, his valet."

"You wouldn't know why he's hired a Pinkerton, would you?"

Dennison shrugged, still smiling gracefully. "I'm not at liberty to say, sir. Are you quite comfortable?"

"Yeah, more'n most, I reckon."

Dennison frowned at the tone of the big man's voice. "Was there something that you lack, sir?"

Raider sized up the valet. Short, slender, gray hairs sprinkled in a thin head of dark hair. Maybe older than he looked, or not as old. Hard to tell what was really inside a man like this, a man who served others.

"Dennison, you think you could find me a carriage?"

The man nodded. "When and where would you be requiring a coach, sir?"

"One hour, in front o' the hotel."

A slight bow from the manservant. "As you wish, sir."

Raider frowned. "Call me by my name, Dennison. Hell, the way you're goin', you're gonna sir me t' death."

"Very good, sir. What shall I call you?" He frowned, like he was in pain.

Raider grimaced, realizing that it was a losing battle. "Don't fret over it, Dennison. Just have that buggy waitin' in one hour."

"Very good, sir."

Dennison disappeared down the hallway. Raider closed the door, wondering if John Sanders was as proper as his butler. What the hell did Sanders need with an agent like Raider anyway? One of Pinkerton's gray-suited dandies would have served him better.

He decided not to think about it until he knew why he had been summoned. Until that moment, he planned to enjoy himself. A night in San Francisco awaited him. Best to have a few more drinks before he got started.

The coach moved slowly along the dark waterfront. Raider sat next to the driver, watching the doorways. The only thing to light their way was the glow from the carriage's side lamps. Raider just couldn't bring himself to get in, so he rode next to the small, chubby man who held the reins.

"You sure you want to be down here, cowpoke?" The driver's voice was tight. He had never been to the waterfront before. The docks would have made anyone nervous, especially at night. Who could tell what might be hiding in the deep shadows. He wanted to go back to the hotel. "This ain't too smart, cowboy. Not on a Saturday night."

Raider waved him off. "I ain't no cowboy. An' just keep that horse movin' slow."

"What the hell are you lookin' for?"

"I'll know when I see it," Raider replied.

He was looking for a special kind of door, one that seemed to be half open, with a candle burning deep inside. There'd be a flight of stairs and a man with some kind of weapon. But the fun would be at the top of the stairs if you could find the place.

"I'm scared, mister," the driver intoned.

Raider gave him a half dollar and told him to shut up.

They rode a few more blocks before Raider saw the doorway and told the driver to stop.

"What are you lookin' at, mister?"

Raider needed to watch the doorway for a while. "What time is it, Jasper?"

"Nine o'clock."

That wasn't really late for a Saturday night, so if the doorway was the place Raider wanted, there would be traffic both ways.

"My wife'll kill me if she finds out I been down here," the driver offered.

Raider gave him a paper dollar.

Somebody came out of the doorway. He stopped, looked up both sides of the street and waddled off toward town. Another man came soon enough and entered the place. This was it.

Raider started to climb off the carriage seat.

"Hey," the driver whined, "where are you goin'?"

"In there," Raider replied, pointing to the shadowy doorway. "If I'm not out in an hour, leave without me."

"But—"

Raider tossed him a five dollar gold piece. "One hour."

"Oh, all right."

"You got a gun?"

The driver nodded.

Raider checked his own boot, making sure his Colt was there on the right side. San Francisco constables didn't really take kindly to a man wearing a side arm. Best to keep the gun nearby but out of sight.

He approached the doorway, listening for sounds of life inside. He heard a man singing in a low, spectral voice. The candle flickered a silhouette against the wall. It looked a little bit like the old entrance to Madam Wu's place.

Raider eased the door open.

An old, black man looked up at him, startling at the hulking shadow that hung in the threshold. He had grayish hair and a harmless face. Raider didn't even see a gun on him.

"Scared the devil out of me," the man said, grimacing.

Raider tipped back his Stetson. "I don't reckon you'd know if one o' Madam Wu's girls is still operatin' in these parts?"

The man's brow fretted. He smiled a little. "Madam Wu. Now there's a name I ain't heard in some time. She was killed a while back."

"I know," Raider replied. "I was there."

"You was? Huh. Lots of trouble back then. It's better now, only you got to go south if you want a real good time."

Raider leaned toward the old man, holding out a dollar. "What chance I got of havin' a good time right here?"

He took the dollar. "If you knowed Madam Wu, then you must know the girl who took her place."

Raider grimaced. "You got me there, honcho. I knew her. Chinese girl. Had a few good times with her an' this blonde. I think the blonde is called Goldie, but for the life o' me, I can't remember that Chinese girl's name."

"Wan Chur," replied the old man. "Top of the stairs. She's got a good head on her, so she might even remember you."

"Raider? Is it really you?"

When the big man nodded, Wan Chur threw her arms around him. She had put on weight since the last time he saw her, and she was pale, like she hadn't seen the sun for a while.

"Wan Chur, you look like you been smokin' that pipe o' yours."

She shrugged, turning away. "Maybe. What brings you back to the waterfront? Don't tell me, let me guess. You want some pussy!"

Raider grinned. "Since you put it like that—"

Wan Chur said that she was no longer in the business herself, except for handling other girls. "Things have gone downhill since you were here the last time, Raider. I just don't have the touch like Madam Wu. We all still miss her a lot. Business hasn't been that great."

Raider took out a wad of cash. "It's about t' pick up. Let me have a look at your girls."

"You'll have a good selection," she replied. "It's been a slow night."

She called out into various rooms, summoning her females. Raider didn't recognize any of the girls. He chose a beautiful Chinese woman with clear eyes and a blonde girl.

"Just like that night you spent with me and Goldie," Wan Chur offered.

Raider drew in a breath that burned deep with his desire.

"What room you want?" Wan Chur asked.

Raider smelled their perfume. It was all he could do to restrain himself, but he didn't want to stay on the waterfront, not all night.

"Honey," he said to Wan Chur, "how much extra will it cost me t' take 'em back t' my hotel?"

She glanced sideways at him. "I don't want my girls staying in some fleabag with you."

"The Grandview ain't no fleabag."

Wan Chur nodded appreciatively. "What'd you do? Strike a vein?"

"How much?"

She waved him off. "Fifty bucks. And you make sure they get back here safe and sound."

Raider put his arms around the girls' shoulders. "Safe an' sound."

They giggled as he rushed them down the stairs.

"See you found what you was lookin' for," said the old black man.

"Night, Jasper. You watch your back."

"Yeah and they gonna be watchin' your front, cowboy!"

Raider laughed as they approached the carriage.

"Ooh, fancy," said the blonde girl.

"I seen better," the Chinese woman rejoined.

The driver gaped at Raider. "You're full of surprises, mister. You want to go back to the hotel?"

Raider opened the door of the coach. "As fast as you can get us there."

The driver frowned at him. "Didn't you bring one of them girls for me?"

"You're a married man," Raider reminded him. "Your wife would kill you if she knew you were in this part o' town."

He lifted the girls into the coach and then climbed in behind them.

"I like riding in coaches, " the blonde said, switching seats so she could sit next to Raider.

"I can take it or leave it," the Chinese girl said.

Raider gave the blonde woman a little peck on the cheek. "You look pretty t'night, darlin'. An' you smell so good."

She kissed him, immediately putting her hand on his crotch.

"Well diddle me!" the blonde cried as she massaged his prick. "What kind of gun you got in there?"

"That ain't no gun," Raider replied. "I'm just glad t' see you."

The Chinese girl scoffed. "Shit. He hasn't got any more than other men. Take it out."

The blonde girl fiddled with the buttons of Raider's pants. She freed the swelling member between his legs, watching it flop about as if it had a life of its own. Raider reached to pull down the shades that covered the coach windows. No need to let the police see him having a good time.

"God, there must be ten inches," the blonde said.

The Chinese girl had switched seats to join them. "God, it is big. Here, let me see it."

"I was here first."

Raider put his arms around both of them. "Don't fight, ladies. We got all night t' fuss over each other. I even got a bathtub in my room."

The blonde began to stroke him up and down. "How's that feel, cowboy?"

"Name's Raider. An' it feels great."

"Huh. I can do better," the Chinese girl challenged.

Blondy didn't want to be outdone. "Cannot!"

They both started to stroke him.

Raider leaned back, wondering if he was going to pay in Hell for this sinful dream. He figured it didn't really matter. And there was no chance of him stopping, not now.

"I'm gonna suck it," the blonde said, dropping toward the tip of his cock.

The Chinese girl started to lower her face. "No, I will."

They were both surprised when Raider's prick exploded, spraying them with a shower of delight.

"Hey," Blondy said, "why'd you do that?"

Raider felt light as air. "Just couldn't help m'self." He was smiling.

The Chinese girl stuffed his soft member back into his pants. "Well," she groaned, "I guess you're through for the night."

Raider put his hand on her thigh. "Not by a long shot, honey. Not by a long shot."

"Excuse me, sir," called the desk clerk. "Where do you think you're going with those two—ladies?"

Raider glared at the clerk. Not the same man who had checked him in. He'd have to dig into his pocket again.

"Let's go talk t' the man," he said to the girls.

The desk clerk trembled when Raider got closer. "Are you a guest of this hotel, sir?"

"Room three-fourteen," Raider replied. "I'm a friend o' Mr. John Sanders. Is that all right with you?"

The man checked the register. "Your name is Raider?"

"None other. And these are my cousins. This is cousin Blondy and this is cousin Chinee. They come t' keep me comp'ny."

The clerk still wasn't ready to go along with him. "I'm sorry, sir, but our hotel policy does not allow unmarried men and women to spend the night here. If you would be so kind as to—"

Raider showed him a five dollar gold piece. "You wanna take a look at the rules again?"

"I could lose my job—"

Another five dollars satisfied him.

Raider turned with the girls and started for the stairs. "Let's go have a drink an' a bath. How 'bout it, girls?"

They both pressed against him.

"Did you see how he handled that jackass?" the blonde woman asked.

"He must be rich," said the Chinese girl. "Hey, cowboy. You ever think about gettin' married?"

Raider laughed. "No. An' I sure as hell don't plan t' think 'bout it. Not ever. Not never. You hear me? Not never."

They laughed all the way to Raider's room.

CHAPTER TEN

"Hey, it's my turn!"

The Chinese girl slapped Raider on the ass. He was on top of the blonde woman, shaking the springs of the fancy bed. If one woman could be trouble, two made things almost impossible.

"Come on, let me back in bed!"

The blonde protested. "I'm not finished yet. Keep on, cowboy. I'm almost there. I haven't felt like this with any man. Ohh—don't stop with that big thing. Don't give up."

Raider felt inclined to obey her. He preferred the blonde anyway. She was bigger than the Oriental girl and she didn't complain as much.

"That's it, cowboy. Oh my God. Oh my God."

Raider felt his own sap rising. He drove his cock as deep as it would go inside her. The blonde whore began to tremble, finding a release of her own. Raider kissed her, grinding as she writhed under him.

"That was good, cowboy. Let's do it again."

The Chinese girl slapped him on the ass. "No fair! I want it now. I got all hot watching you two."

Raider rolled off the blonde, frowning at the dark-skinned Eastern beauty. "I ain't finished yet."

She grabbed his wet cock. "Yes you are. Look at this. You came twice since we left the docks. You won't be hard again for a week."

Raider knew better. But he wanted to string things along, that way the Chinese girl would appreciate it more when she finally got it. Let her sweat in the meantime.

Raider put his hands behind his head, leaning back on the pillows. "Mebbe y'all could do it with each other," he suggested.

The Chinese girl frowned. "What do you mean?"

He grinned at her. "Aw, come on now, honey. I know what goes on in cathouses. Hell, y'all get so sick o' men you start t' takin' up with one another. Ain't that right?"

"To hell with you!"

The blonde girl sat up beside him. "Oh, you know he's tellin' the truth. We've done it before."

The Oriental girl turned away, pouting.

Raider gestured to the blonde. "Go on, comfort her. She needs it."

The blonde got off the bed and put her arms around the Chinese girl. "Get in bed with me, honey. It may make him hot. And I know you want some of that big thing. It sure as hell took the edge off for me."

"Yeah," Raider said. "Come on. There's room for all of us."

She called him a cotton-dick cowboy, but she got into bed.

Raider watched as the two women began to kiss. He knew it was the kind of spectacle that could doom a man to the fires of Hell, but he just couldn't resist. The Chinese girl got hotter as the blonde fiddled between the soft skin of her dark thighs.

"You know just where to touch me."

The blonde rolled her eyes at Raider. "You ready yet?"

He shook his head. "It may take a while."

He had to roll under the sheet so they couldn't see that he was getting hard again.

The Chinese girl spread out on her back, lifting her legs a little. "Kiss me down there, honey. Just a little."

The blonde dipped her head between the girl's legs, lapping at the wet crevice of her cunt, driving her mad.

Raider couldn't resist anymore. He pushed the blonde away and fell on top of the Oriental girl. She quickly guided the head of his big cock to the moist entrance of her vagina.

"I want it all," she said. "But slow. And don't fuck me hard unless I tell you to."

Raider eased into her, stopping when she told him to take it easy.

"Doesn't it feel good?" the blonde asked.

The Oriental girl nodded. "I want it," she murmured. "But keep it slow until—ohh—"

Raider ignored her request, thrusting in and out of her. She wrapped her legs around his waist, hanging on for the ride. The bed was shaking so much that the blonde had to climb off.

"He sure knows how to fuck," she said, feeling her own desire starting to rekindle.

The Chinese girl's eyes rolled up. "Stop. Please. Just stop."

Raider hesitated before he started to pull out.

"No," she said, "leave it in there. Just don't move."

Raider tried to hold still but he couldn't remain motionless.

The girl looked up at him when he started to hump again. "Let me get on top," she pleaded. "I want to sit on your prick."

"You won't regret it, cowboy," the blonde intoned. "Let her do it."

Raider figured the girls had earned a favor. He rolled off her, lying back on the mattress. Immediately the dark body was hovering over him. She guided the head of his prick to her wet entrance.

"Now I'm going to fuck you silly!"

Her tight ass started to move, working his cock inside her. At first Raider wondered if she would evoke another release from him. Her hips were slow, deliberate as she took her own pleasure.

"Hurry up," the blonde said, "I want it again."

Raider had gotten himself into something of a mess. But he just lay there, unable to retreat. It felt sort of sinful, but he knew the memory would sustain him the next time he was on the trail.

The Chinese girl picked up the gyrating action of her hips. She took him all the way, sitting down until her ass bumped against his testicles. His cock started to swell with another burst of hot climax. He reached up, pulling her down where he could kiss her.

When he erupted, the milky discharge spilled out between the lips of her cunt. She made him stay in for a while. But the blonde was already anxious to get back into bed.

"I want it again," she said.

"Oh, wait your turn," the Chinese girl replied.

Raider rolled her off him. "Y'all are gonna have t' give me a break, girls. Let's have a couple shots o' whiskey."

"I want to fuck again," the blonde said.

"Yeah, fuck her again, cowboy."

Raider shook his head. "Not till I've had a couple shots o' that hooch over there."

He strode across the room, picking up the bottle of Canadian whiskey.

The women saw that they weren't going to get their way, so they decided to join him. After a couple of belts, Raider was telling them about his life as a detective and they told him about whoring.

"I've never loved a man," the Chinese girl boasted. "Not even my own father. And I never will."

The blonde ran her hands across Raider's shoulders. "Not even a big handsome buck like this one?"

"Ha!" She made a spitting noise. "He's the worst kind. Oh, he might top you pretty good. And you might have some good times with him. But then when his pecker has had enough, he's on his horse again, riding the hell away from you."

Raider swallowed some of the smooth liquid. "Yeah, I'm a real turd in the pasture. Been that way since I can remember."

"Aw, she's just bitter," the blonde girl replied. "Besides, I wouldn't want no man that would stay in a place like San Francisco. Hell, he'd just have to get work and live in a house with me. Before I knew it, he wouldn't be the kind of man I'd want anymore."

"You're both right," the big man offered. "Now, what say we use that bathtub in the other room? I don't know about y'all, but I'm kinda sweaty."

The three of them all fit in the tub together. They splashed until Raider's swelling member poked through the surface of the murky water. Then the girls wanted to get into bed again.

They didn't even dry their bodies. The blonde took her turn and then the Chinese girl straddled his crotch. Raider couldn't come, but it didn't matter. He was hard and that was all it took to satisfy his bedmates. When they had both had their fill, they sank into the mattress, laughing for a while, and then drifted off to sleep.

Raider didn't wake until he heard the key in the door to his room. Somebody was trying to enter quietly. He reached for the Colt, which always hung on the post of the bed where he was sleeping. He thumbed back the hammer and waited for the door to open.

Raider slid off the bed, aiming the Colt at the threshold.

It was morning and the unexpected brightness caused his vision to blur. At first, he thought he was seeing things. A woman's hat, fresh with colorful plumes, came through the doorway.

Then he thought he heard her laughing at him.

He focused on the beautiful creature who stared at him with wide blue eyes. How the hell had she gotten through the door? He considered shooting her but she didn't seem to be offering any threat.

"I just wanted to see what a Pinkerton agent looked like," she said in a husky voice. "My word, you've got two large pistols."

Raider scowled at her, keeping the gun in front of him. "Who the hell are you?"

She seemed to disregard his question. "I bribed the bellhop to let me in. He didn't act very surprised that you were expecting a woman. And now I see why." She nodded to the two women in Raider's bed. "My, my, you have such an appetite."

Her blue eyes focused on his dangling member.

Raider gestured with the pistol. "Get the hell outta here."

She hesitated, locking her gaze on his black eyes. Pretty brown hair pushed up under the feathery hat. Narrow waist, healthy chest. Smooth face with a little more rouge than Raider liked. He was starting to get aroused.

Her thick lips parted and she gave a little gasp. "A pity I can't stay. Perhaps we'll see each other again."

Raider waved the barrel of the Colt. "Go on, afore I—"

"Madam! Honestly!"

Dennison, the butler, came in behind the pretty woman.

She winked at Raider. "Duty calls."

Dennison blushed as the woman brushed past him.

Raider lowered the weapon. "Who the hell was that?"

"Mrs. John Sanders!" Dennison replied.

The big man's jaw went slack. "Whoa!"

The butler glanced at the bed. "My word!"

Raider shrugged it off. "Ain't nothin'. Just a couple o' cousins who didn't have no place t' sleep."

Dennison waved his hands in front of him. "It doesn't matter. Mr. Sanders is waiting for you."

"He ain't gonna wanna see me, not after his wife saw me in the raw."

"Don't worry about madam. She won't cause as much trouble as you might think. She's very much like me, one of the trappings of Mr. Sanders's life. Now hurry along. He's next door, in room three-fifteen."

The whole thing puzzled Raider. The butler didn't seem fazed by the woman's lewdness. And now he wanted the big man to see his boss.

Dennison started into the hall.

"Hey, honcho, how 'bout gettin' these two ladies back home for me? Make sure they ain't hurt."

"Sir, I—"

Raider reached for his pants. "They ain't gonna bite you, Dennison. And if you wanna take a turn with 'em—"

"Sir! I should hardly think that would be appropriate!"

Raider glared at him. "You gonna tell your boss 'bout the woman there? I mean, I was in my birthday suit."

"My job is to spare Mr. Sanders the pain of her brashness. You'll see; it isn't as bad as it looks. She takes care of Mr. Sanders in certain ways."

"I'll bet she does."

Dennison smiled at him. It seemed like a cold expression, even though his lips were wearing a grin. That was what being a servant did to you, Raider thought. He felt sort of bad about the way he had been acting since he arrived at the hotel. It just wasn't right to act snotty and stupid.

"Dennison, if I was rough t' you, I'm sorry."

A wave from the butler. "Oh, don't let it bother you, sir. I learned my job well in England. I spent five years there, working for a nobleman. Of course, I was homesick and decided to return to my native California. I was lucky enough to sign on with Mr. Sanders."

"Stay close," Raider told him. "I might need your help."

"Very good, sir."

Dennison left him to get ready. Raider had to admit that he kind of liked the dandified bulter. Dennison reminded him of his old partner, Doc Weatherbee. If you considered the blue-eyed woman, Raider was already running into strange characters. He found himself anxious to meet John Sanders, the man who had orchestrated everything so far.

John Sanders was a wiry, rugged-looking pug of a man who looked as if he had always taken the rough road. He was somewhere between forty and fifty years of age with little gray in his dark head of hair. The age showed in his tanned face. The rest of him seemed pretty fit as he paced back and forth in front of Raider. The big man sat in a plush chair, trying to feel comfortable in his new clothes. The collar scratched his neck.

Sanders had been lecturing Raider on his career in California, how he had built up his ranch near Stockton, taking it from dirt to cattle, making a fortune in the process. He spoke in a clear, gruff voice, as if he was not used to anyone questioning his authority.

"So you see, Mr. Raider, when John Sanders hires a Pinkerton, well, you've just been hired by one of the most influential men in this state."

Raider nodded, trying not to look at the woman who sat across from him on the other side of the room, perched seductively on the edge of the big bed. Raider knew that she was along for the ride. The old man had money and he seemed to be in good enough shape to keep her reasonably happy in the sack. Raider hoped she didn't get in the way if he took the case.

"Now," Sanders said finally, turning to regard him with clear gray eyes. "I'll want you to start for me at once."

Raider winced. He heard the same tone that he had been using since he had arrived at the Grandview. He didn't like being talked down to, like he was some servant.

Sanders clapped his hands. "Dennison, take—"

Raider waved off the butler, which made Dennison smile.

Mrs. Sanders was smiling too.

"Now hold on, Sanders," Raider said. "S'pose you tell me what you hired me for. I'd like to hear it outright afore I take the case."

Sanders glared at the tall Pinkerton. "*Before* you take the case? Listen, I hired you and I expect—"

Raider stood up. "I'm afraid I'll have t' go, Mr. Sanders. See, if you won't tell me what I been hired t' do, then I'll have t' send a wire t' the home office. I can refuse any case I see fit. It's a bargain I struck with my bosses."

Sanders pointed a finger at him. "I'm your boss now."

"Not unless I officially accept the case. Until then, I'm ready t' listen."

Sanders nodded, offering him the chair again. "All right. Sit down."

Raider took his seat.

"I want you to escort my wife back to Stockton," Sanders offered. "Is that enough for you?"

Raider exhaled, shaking his head. "I'm 'fraid not."

Mrs. Sanders laughed from across the room. "You better watch your step, Mr. Pinkerton. Did you know that Johnny is one of the most powerful men in this part of the state? Why, he's running for mayor of Stockton."

Raider frowned at the leathery old gent. "Sorry, Mr. Sanders. My agency don't take t' gettin' locked up in politics."

Sanders sighed. "The task I've hired you for has nothing to do with my political campaign. Please hear me out."

"Only if you're gonna tell me ever'thin'. I don't like surprises, Mr. Sanders. Surprises can get you killed."

Sanders looked at his wife. "Ellen, would you leave us for a moment?"

She shrugged and slid off the bed. "I was getting bored, anyway."

"Thank you."

Ellen Sanders paused long enough to put her arms around her husband's shoulders. She pecked him on the cheek and begged him not to send her back to Stockton alone. She always got so frightened when she rode in a stagecoach by herself.

"I'll see to it, dear."

When she was out of the room, Sanders smiled weakly at Raider. "I must offer you my apologies for both of us, Mr. Raider."

"Just Raider."

Sanders nodded slightly. "This territory has changed so much since I first came here. I forget that there are still men like you, Raider."

"How's that?"

"You're one of the few men left who won't let another man

push you around in the name of money. I can see why Mr. Pinkerton sent you to me."

Raider folded his arms. "All I wanna know is why you really hired me."

Sanders frowned, rubbing his chin. He seemed like a man about to make a confession. Searching for the words.

He finally turned to Raider and asked for his gun.

The big man grimaced. "Come again?"

"Let me see your gun," Sanders replied. "A forty-four, isn't it? I want to show you something."

Raider hesitated with his hand on the redwood grip of the Colt. "What d' you need my gun for?"

"Nothing dangerous, I can assure you. Go ahead and take the bullets out of the chamber if it will make you more comfortable."

Raider unloaded the Colt and handed it to Sanders.

The old gentleman went through some moves that made Raider sit up straight in his chair. Sanders spun the Colt on his finger, caught the handle and thumbed back the hammer. He let it fall on an empty chamber and then did the same move with his left hand.

He tossed the Colt back and forth, stopping it to pop out the cylinder and spin the wheel.

Raider held his breath when Sanders tossed the weapon into the air. It flipped twice before he caught it and clicked the hammer again.

"Good balance," he said. "Watch this."

Sanders went behind his back spinning the gun over his left shoulder, grabbing the redwood handle in his left hand.

It was all a little too showy, but Raider was still impressed. "So, you know how t' handle a gun. What's that mean t' me?"

Sanders gave him back the Colt. "It's a secret, Raider. A secret that could ruin me. I've come too far for this to happen now and I'm hoping you can stop it for me. You see, I wasn't always a gentleman. And sometimes I still find it hard to do the right thing."

Raider leaned back in the chair. "You gonna make this long, Sanders? Or can you just come out an' tell me?"

"All right, I'll get to the point."

He took a deep breath and then asked Raider if he had ever heard of Johnny Sonora.

• • •

Raider gawked at Sanders. He shouldn't have been surprised at the question, not the way things usually went for him on a case. Pinkerton and Wagner always assigned him to the strange ones.

"Are you talkin' 'bout that punk they call the California Kid?"

Sanders nodded. "That's him."

Raider straightened in the chair. "I ran into him way north o' here, up at Yreka. He's pretty fast with a gun." Almost as fast as me, he said to himself.

"So he's really as fast as they say?"

Raider's eyes narrowed. "Why would a man like you be int'rested in Johnny Sonora? What's he t' you?"

Sanders took in a deep breath. "He is *me*."

"Come again?"

Sanders slumped into a chair opposite Raider. "I figured you wouldn't believe what I'm about to say unless you saw me handle the gun."

Raider nodded. "You were fair. Can you shoot?"

Sanders looked up at him. "I was one of the best. I went by the name Johnny Sonora. I was called the California Kid."

Raider whistled."That musta been a while back. I mean—hey, wait a minute. You went by the same name as that boy I saw in Yreka?"

"Almost thirty years ago," Sanders offered. "Before the war. During the first gold rush. I had a name. A reputation. I killed a man named Mule Gallagher and after that, well, I don't suppose I have to tell a man in your line of work how a reputation grows."

Raider shrugged. "Sometimes you don't even have t' earn it. Did you earn your reputation, Sanders?"

"I killed men. But I never shot anybody that wasn't trying to shoot me. I never robbed anyone either. I admit that I drank and chased women. Don't tell my wife I said that."

Raider figured Mrs. Sanders wouldn't be offended, but he didn't say it out loud. He found himself drawn to Sanders. A former gunfighter who had made good—if he was telling the truth. He wanted to know more about the man.

"Mr. Sanders, if you didn't rob no one, how'd you get so rich?"

"The war," Sanders replied. "I was a good soldier. Quickly rose to the rank of captain. I served for a while in the west. I was a major when I left the army. That was when I bought my ranch and started to raise cattle. I told you the rest."

Raider shook his head, sighing. "An' I thought I heard it all."

Sanders gaped at him. "You don't believe me?"

"I ain't sure what t' b'lieve," the big man replied. "Afore I met you an' that boy in Yreka, I had knowed three men who used the name the California Kid. I killed two of 'em, an' as I recall, the other one was killed by somebody else. You got anythin' t' prove you was who you say you was?"

Sanders nodded. "I knew you'd want proof. Here, look through this trunk. See if this will satisfy you."

Sanders had it all in chronological order. He had clippings about gunfights that he had been in as Johnny Sonora. All fair fights, according to the press. He had things from the war, pictures of him in different uniforms as he had risen in rank.

Raider still didn't get the point. "What does all this have t' do with me, Sanders?"

"Don't you see? This kid has surfaced, using my old name."

"Mebbe it's just a coincidence."

"Both names?" Sanders challenged. "I think not."

Raider stretched out his legs. "What d' you want me t' do 'bout it?"

"Find out who's behind this kid," Sanders replied. "See if it's a plot to discredit me in my race for mayor."

Raider held up his hands. "Now hold on, I can't get involved in that politick-stumpin'."

"No one is asking you to," Sanders offered. "Just track down this kid and find out why he's using my old name. You can do that, can't you?"

"I s'pose. Mebbe he's broken the law, too. Although, he's just like you were in one thing."

Sanders frowned. "What's that?"

"When he killed those two men in Yreka, it was a fair fight. They drew first an' Sonora got 'em both. He's fast."

Sanders bit his knuckle. "I knew it. I tell you, this has something to do with me. Why did this kid turn up just now?"

"I wouldn't worry too much," Raider said, "I mean, he's north o' here right now, a good piece away from you."

"I still don't like it, Raider. I tell you what. I'll strike a deal with you. You take the case and I'll promise you that you will in no way be involved in my race for mayor of Stockton."

"Shake on it."

They clasped hands. Raider figured there wasn't anything wrong with poking around to see what he could learn about the new Johnny Sonora. He had to document some of Sanders's claims. He could always back out of the case if the old gent tried to pull him into the politics.

"Just one more thing," Sanders said. "I really would appreciate it if you would accompany my wife back to Stockton."

"I'd like t' get started soon as possible," Raider replied.

"Please," Sanders entreated. "It would make me feel a whole lot better."

Raider finally agreed to do it. He figured he could talk to the wife for a while and then strike out on his own. He wondered what the woman would have to say. He didn't take her for the shy kind. Not by a long shot.

CHAPTER ELEVEN

When he got back to his room, Raider found Mrs. Ellen Sanders lying on the bed. "I had the maid change the sheets," she said, grinning.

Raider turned his shoulder to her. "We're due on a stage outta here at one o'clock, lady. You better get packed."

She shrugged. "Oh, Dennison will take care of that. He's really a wonder. John is lucky to have him. And me too."

"I'll bet."

He started to repack his saddle bags, shifting things, throwing things away. He'd have to leave the gray, maybe even sell it. Unless he doubled back to San Francisco, he'd have to buy another mount in Stockton. Best to sell the gray. If he was going off after Johnny Sonora, he wouldn't have any time to waste. He wondered if there was anything to the story Sanders had told him. He'd have to turn over the rock to see what was really beneath it.

"Hey!" Mrs. Sanders said. "You ignoring me?"

Raider gestured toward the door. "We'll talk on the coach."

"Who says I came to talk?"

She leaned forward, throwing a kiss in his direction.

Raider rolled his eyes. "Just as long as you ain't obvious."

She frowned playfully. "Oh, don't tell me I'm not going to

have any fun! Why, those girls spoke highly of you before they left here."

Raider was about to tell her that she had gone too far when the rapping of knuckles on the door interrupted them.

Raider grinned at Mrs. Sanders. "Let's hope it ain't your hubby. Come on in!"

Dennison opened the door and looked in. "Oh, I'm sorry I—"

"It's okay," Raider replied. "Mrs. Sanders was about t' leave anyway."

She climbed off the bed. "You're no fun at all."

"Be at the depot afore one," Raider told her. "I'll meet you there."

Mrs. Sanders paused at the door. "I prefer trains, if you want to know the truth. The stagecoach will let us off right at the ranch. See you later, Mr. Pinkerton." She winked and slid into the hall.

Dennison shook his head. "Allow me to apologize for her."

Raider's brow fretted. "Don't your boss know 'bout her?"

"I've never asked," Dennison replied.

"How long you been with Sanders?"

"Eight months, sir."

"How long has he been married t' the lady?"

Dennison shrugged. "She was here when I arrived."

"An' he's never told you how long he's been married to her?"

The butler stiffened proudly. "Sir, to be a good servant, one must never go beyond one's bounds. If your employer offers information of his private life, you consider it confidential. Otherwise, you must assume that his private affairs are none of your business."

"All right," Raider challenged, "but holdin' back may get your boss in a bunch o' trouble."

Dennison's face slacked and for a moment Raider saw a strange expression on the man's countenance.

"Just keep that in mind, Dennison. An' watch your boss's back."

Raider waited to see if the butler would offer any confessions, but Dennison remained quiet.

He tipped his Stetson to the man, gathering his gear. "Got chores t' take care of afore I leave, Dennison. If you change your mind, meet me at the stage depot later on."

"I assure you, Mr. Raider, that I cannot help you in any way."

The big man stepped into the hall. He had business at the livery. He hoped he could get a good price for the gray. He hated having to sell a good horse. It was almost like a bad omen. He shook off the coldness in his shoulders and started for the stairs.

The stage rolled out of San Francisco promptly at one o'clock. Raider and Mrs. Sanders sat opposite each other on the coach's plush leather seats. She wore a mischievous expression on her face, like she had something in mind. Raider ignored her, sliding sideways on the seat, reclining with his legs bent. At first he pretended to sleep and then he nodded off for a long time.

When he woke up, the woman was still in her seat, smiling at him. He wondered if she had been napping while he was out. Shouldn't have slept so long, he thought. The previous night had left him without much strength.

"You slept while we stopped in Stockton. We're almost to Green Sands," Mrs. Sanders offered.

Raider sat upright, straightening his hat. "Where?"

"Green Sands," she repeated. "That's the name of our ranch. Don't ask me how it got that incredible name because I don't know."

"Can I get a horse there?"

She shrugged. "We've got plenty. Take whatever you need. I know you're off to do some dastardly deed for John."

"How d' you know that?"

She smirked. "Men. Politics. It's all the same game. John hires his errand boys—"

"I work for the Pinkerton National Detective Agency," Raider said, cutting her off. "I ain't nobody's errand boy."

"What's that supposed to mean?"

Raider saw a glimmer of doubt in her eyes. "It means that I don't take sides when I come into somethin'. Not till I have all the worms in one can. An' no matter who's wrong, I have t' stick t' the truth. You get me?"

She put a hand to her throat. "I can assure you that there's nothing wrong. Do you hear *me*?"

Raider shrugged. "Then you ain't got nothin' t' worry 'bout."

The coach continued on, bumping into the night. Darkness didn't seem to deter the carriage driver. Raider had to bang on the roof to get him to stop for a while. When everything had been relieved, including his thirst, he got back into the carriage.

The driver started up again, heading for the Sanders ranch.

Raider asked Mrs. Sanders how much longer before they reached Green Sands.

"Another hour," she replied. "And please, call me Ellen."

Raider saw the move coming.

Her thick lips parted slightly. "You know, I like to get to know all of John's men on a personal basis. Perhaps we could—"

She started over to his side of the coach.

Raider put his hand on her chest and pushed her back. "Sorry," he said. "Reckon we hit a chuckhole back there."

She didn't seem that disappointed. "Yes, I suppose we did."

He thought it was the right time to attack. He shook his head, chuckling to himself. He kept it up until she couldn't stand it anymore.

Mrs. Sanders gawked at him. "What?"

"Dog me, I can't figger you out, Mrs. Sanders."

She smiled a little at that comment. Women loved it when you talked about them. And they liked it even better when you listened to them talk about themselves.

"What can't you figure out about me?"

Raider leaned back in the seat. "Well, you look an' talk like one o' them high society women, the kind who live in the rich neighborhoods in San Francisco. But you act like one o' the girls I found down at the docks. Which is it?"

She raised an eyebrow. "I assure you that my family is one of the foremost in San Francisco."

"That where you met Sanders?"

"He called on me the way a proper gentleman calls on a widow. We courted for six months before I decided to marry him."

Raider wasn't surprised to hear she had buried one husband already. "How'd your first husband die?"

"Just keeled over." She made a gesture with her hand. "But it's not what you're thinking. I didn't get a dime of inheritance. His family got everything. But then, I suppose you'll find all that out when you start to pry into my background."

That had caught him off guard. "What are you talkin' 'bout?"

"Isn't that what John has hired you to do? To spy on me?"

Raider laughed. "You got a real high opinion o' yourself, Mrs. Sanders."

She stiffened a little. "In answer to your other inquiry, Raider,

I like to have a good time as much as any woman. I'm not innocent anymore, although I look younger than I really am. Fancy ladies, as you would call them, need diversions too."

Raider waved a hand in front of her, a final gesture. "I don't make a habit o' foolin' 'round with the wives o' the men who hire me, Mrs. Sanders. Now I wanna help your husband, an' if you wanna help him too, you'll cooperate with me. Think you can do that?"

She pouted, raising a handkerchief in front of her face.

Raider thought she seemed a little too guilty about something. Maybe she was behind the scheme to defame her husband. If there was a scheme in motion.

"You're bored, ain't you, Mrs. Sanders?"

"Yes, but I'm comfortable," she replied.

When he considered it more closely, he wondered what she would have to gain by discrediting her husband. Sanders seemed to give her free rein to do whatever she wanted. Hell, she was part of the masquerade, like the fancy-talking butler. Sanders, former hired gun, made good in the army and wants to be mayor of Stockton.

He was going to start in on her again, but the carriage slowed for an unexpected stop. "Is this the ranch?" he asked.

Mrs. Sanders shook her head. "No. It's too soon. This is the station before the ranch."

Raider opened the door and climbed out of the carriage. "What's wrong?" he called to the driver.

The shotgun rider looked down at him. "The lights ain't on in the station," the man replied.

Raider frowned, peering into darkness. "Is that the usual way?"

"No, sir. Pete's always got a light on at the station. And he knows what time we come in."

Raider climbed up behind them, but he still couldn't see the cabin in the distance. What if the man had simply forgot to put a match to the lantern? The driver said Pete never forgot. There had to be something wrong.

"Okay," the big man said. "Here's what we have t' do. First, we get the woman outta there. One of you stay with her. Now listen, the next part is real tricky—"

• • •

The stagecoach driver bent down, peering beneath the vehicle. "I sure hope this works, Pinkerton."

Raider clung to the undercarriage, balanced on the chassis. "Just take it slow an' do like I told you."

The driver glanced back into the shadows, where the shotgun rider stood with Mrs. Sanders. It had seemed like a good idea, at least until it was time to go. Now he was having second thoughts, even with Raider's Winchester under his seat.

"I ain't sure about this, Pinkerton."

"You ain't the only one," Raider called from beneath the coach. "Keep it slow. An' don't be afraid t' use that rifle I gave you."

The man climbed into the seat, urging the team forward. He had to rein back to keep the horses from running too fast. They could smell the hay and water at the station. They wanted to be resting, to give over the harness to a new team.

Raider bounced around below, trying to keep his balance. They were too close for him to yell out, to tell the driver to slow down. He was moving straight into the ambush, if that was what it was.

The driver reined back at the station, skidding to a stop close to the front door. Raider hung on, glad that the coach was finally still. He and the driver both froze where they were, listening in the darkness.

For a moment, Raider thought his elaborate plan had been in vain. The station man had probably fallen asleep and forgotten to light the lantern. All men made mistakes from time to time. The big man was about to call out to the driver when he heard the rifle levers.

A voice came from the darkness. "Hold it right there."

Blackjack! Raider thought to himself.

His hand slipped down to his boot, drawing the Colt that he had put there earlier. He thumbed back the hammer, listening, waiting for the ambushers to move into range. He didn't have to wait long.

Raider could hear two of them striding toward the coach. They were wearing spurs and long dusters. He could see their legs, but he didn't have the angle for a shot. Not yet, anyway.

"This coach come from San Francisco?" a voice asked.

The driver replied in a low voice. "Yeah, that's where it come from."

"Is the Pinkerton on here?"

Raider flinched. They were looking for *him*. How the hell did they know he was on the coach? Maybe it was some of his colleagues. Wagner sometimes sent men out to look for him.

"Ain't nobody on this coach," the driver replied, just as Raider had told him. "I'm takin' it to Manteca after I change the team."

Another voice rose in the darkness. "We want the Pinkerton. Where the hell is he?"

Raider was sure he had never heard the voices before. He'd recognize the voice of any man Wagner sent after him. These men were strangers. Who the hell had sent them?

"Where'd the Pinkerton get off?"

The driver was silent.

"Answer us, boy. Or I'll blow your head off."

No Pinkerton or lawman would make a threat like that, Raider thought. And any agents looking for him would ask for him by name first. It was never wise to let anyone know you were a Pinkerton right away. These two were hostile.

"Look inside," said one of the bushwhackers.

Raider knew the time was coming. The ambusher walked to the coach door, opening it. Raider saw the torso right in front of him. He pointed the Colt at the man's crotch and squeezed off one shot.

The man hollered terribly, backing up, holding his groin.

Raider dropped to the ground, sliding belly down.

The other man thought the shot had come from inside the coach. He started moving toward the carriage, firing into the cabin. Slugs splintered the wood above Raider, missing him by a couple of feet. The bushwhacker ran into his line of vision, pumping the Winchester as fast as he could shoot.

Raider held the Colt with both hands, taking careful aim. He had a clear shot at the man's head. The gun exploded, sending a slug between the bushwhacker's eyes.

The man staggered backward, twitching as the blood poured from the hole in his forehead.

Raider rolled away from them, coming up on the other side of the carriage.

Somebody moved from above, dropping down.

Raider leveled the Colt at the driver's head.

"It's only me, Pinkerton!" He had Raider's Winchester in hand.

Raider lifted a finger to his mouth. "Shh. I ain't sure I got all of 'em. You stay right here. Back me up while I have a look inside."

Raider eased around behind the carriage, peering toward the station shack. Dark as molasses inside. He moved slowly, tiptoeing toward the door. It swung open with one touch. Raider stepped inside, letting the Colt lead the way. He heard muffled sounds and thrashings. He found the station man tied up across the room. Raider moved over and untied him.

"Was that you shootin'?" the man asked.

Raider told him to be quiet. "An' you stay here till I tell you t' come out. Understand?"

The man nodded.

Raider moved toward the front door. He could not see the driver. He started to call out, but he hesitated.

Easing to the edge of the doorstep, Raider listened for movement. The horses startled a little. That was probably the driver coming around.

He stepped outside. "Your friend is okay in there. He was—"

Raider heard the unmistakable click of a rifle hammer going back.

"Shit!"

The man stood on the roof behind him.

Raider was turning to fire when a rifle exploded.

Only it wasn't the rifle from the roof. The shot had come from behind the coach. The man on the roof doubled over and fell forward, rolling to the ground with a thud.

Raider looked down at the dead man. He was dressed like the others. Stayed back until he had a sure shot. He hadn't been counting on the driver having Raider's Winchester in hand.

The pale driver stepped up beside the big man from Arkansas. He shook his head, looking at the body. "Reckon I got him."

Raider nodded. "Reckon you did at that. I'm obliged t' you for savin' my life, pardner."

"Ain't never killed a man before." He made a gagging noise. "Think I'm gonna be sick."

Raider urged him back into the shadows. "Do what you have t' do, pilgrim. Just don't get any on your boots."

The driver went off to retch by himself.

Raider gazed down at the body. He felt sort of sick himself. But he had work to do. The three men had been after *him*, and he aimed to find out why.

Raider had all three bodies lying next to each other, like dead soldiers before a burial patrol. He had gone through their pockets, finding that each of them had three hundred dollars in new bank notes. The serial numbers were consecutive on the bills, which meant that they had all been paid by the same hand. They also had a few more dollars on them, the regular things a man carried on the trail, and a lot of ammunition.

"They're hired guns," Raider said to the driver. "Leastways, they were."

The man scratched his head. "What did they want with you?"

Raider shrugged. "I don't know, but I have a feelin' they was hired t' kill me. That's where the new money came from."

The driver eyed the wad of money. "Sure is a lot of hay."

"Nine hundred dollars," Raider replied. "Somebody sure wanted me dead."

But did these men have anything to do with the case he was handling at the moment? They could have been hired by somebody to even an old score. Or maybe somebody had gotten scared when John Sanders brought in a Pinkerton.

"I reckon I better go get them other two," the driver said. "They'll be fearin', what with all this shootin'."

Raider stopped him. "Hold on there, honcho. I wanna talk t' you for a second. And get Pete out here too."

The driver called the station man, who came out and stared at the bodies.

"In case y'all ain't noticed," Raider offered, "we got ourselves three dead men here."

The station man balked. "I didn't kill nobody."

Raider waved him off. "Don't worry, pardner. Ain't nobody accusin' you o' nothin'."

The driver tried to swallow. "I killed one of 'em."

"Who killed who ain't the point," Raider went on. "These boys was askin' for it an' we gave it to 'em."

"Y'all sure did," the station man replied.

Raider gazed toward the dark horizon. "Where's the nearest law from here?"

"Stockton," the station man replied.

Raider exhaled, rubbing his chin. "Shame that we have t' go tell the law what happened. Ain't it?"

The driver rolled his eyes. "Don't have t' tell 'em. Do we?"

Raider lifted up the money so they could see it. "No, we don't. But we do have t' share this loot. Here; a hundred for each of you. An' I'll give a hundred t' the shotgun rider. That's fair, ain't it?"

The station man nodded. "Sounds fair to me."

"Course, you'll have t' bury these bodies," Raider offered.

"I can do that," the station man replied. "Hell, they was prob- ably outlaws anyway. Maybe I should take 'em into Stockton for a reward."

"You do whatever you want," Raider said. "They prob'ly got mounts tied 'round here too. Find 'em and they're yours."

The driver eyed the six hundred dollars in Raider's hand. "What're you gonna do with the rest of the cash?"

"Show it to Mr. Sanders," Raider replied. "Now, you run on an' get the others. Don't tell the woman what happened."

"What if she asks why we were shootin'?"

Raider shrugged. "Tell her there was a cougar stalkin' ol' Pete here. We had t' scare it away."

The driver nodded and started for the carriage.

Raider gestured to the bodies. "Come on, we better get 'em 'round back. I don't want the woman t' see 'em."

The station man sighed. "Yeah, that wouldn't be right."

"Just one thing."

"What's that?"

Raider looked the man in the eye. "If you take these men into Stockton, don't say I killed 'em. You play the hero if you want to, but don't tell the sheriff 'bout me."

"No, sir, Mr. Pinkerton. No, sir."

The woman smirked when Raider climbed back into the car- riage. "Did you scare away the pussycat?"

Raider shrugged. "Cougars can be dangerous."

She looked away. "I suppose."

"This cougar had six legs," Raider offered.

The coach lurched forward. The team had been changed for the last leg of the journey. Raider figured they couldn't be far from Sanders's ranch.

"Six legs?" said Mrs. Sanders. "What are you talking about?"

"You don't know?" Raider challenged.

She laughed it off. "You have a strange sense of humor, Mr. Raider."

He just leaned back, lowering the brim of his hat over his eyes.

They hurried on in silence until the driver braked again.

Raider couldn't tell much about the Sanders spread, not in the dark. He was led into a big house, where black servants met the lady of the house. He wondered if Mrs. Sanders would come after him again.

She turned to the big man and waved him toward a flight of steps. "Show this gentleman to his room," she commanded.

Raider hesitated. "Mrs. Sanders, when will your husband be home?"

"Tomorrow morning."

Raider grinned at her. "Good. I have a lot t' tell him."

"Whatever do you mean, Mr. Raider?"

He winked at her and followed the black woman to his room. It was a big chamber, not as fancy as the room in San Francisco, but more to his liking. The driver and the shotgun man came in with his gear.

"Put it in the corner, boys. An' remember; not a word 'bout what happened at the station shack."

"Not even to Mr. Sanders?" the driver asked.

"I'll take care o' him," Raider replied. "Y'all get along afore there's more trouble."

They didn't have to be told twice.

When he was alone, Raider stripped to the waist and took off his boots. The night was warm. He pulled a chair next to an open window and started to think. It wasn't long before his thoughts were disturbed by someone moving below the window.

He was reaching for his Colt when he heard the voice of a woman. She was cursing, like she had stubbed her toe. It sounded like Mrs. Sanders. Raider thought she might be coming to see him, but he finally realized she was moving away. He opened the window and swung out, lowering himself to the ground.

The shadow of the woman's figure seemed to be floating across the yard.

Raider followed her to the edge of a huge barn in the back. Mrs. Sanders stopped behind the barn, like she was waiting for someone. It wasn't long before her guest arrived.

Raider heard them kissing and groping. They even fell to the ground, humping right there. When they were finished, Mrs. Sanders started to talk.

"He's hired someone."

"Shh!" her lover urged. "It doesn't matter. I don't think he suspects us."

She sighed. "I hope not."

Raider had to smile. Mrs. Sanders hadn't even been able to wait an hour before she ran to her lover. He must've known she was on the way home for their rendezvous. And it sounded like they were involved in something besides adultery.

Raider waited for a while longer, until the man was getting ready to go.

"Oh, Franklin," said Mrs. Sanders. "I hope John doesn't find out."

"Don't worry. He won't."

Raider smiled again. He had a name. Franklin. That would come in handy. He started back to the house. Best to get as much sleep as he could before he confronted the lord of the manor. As he had said earlier, the big man from Arkansas sure had a lot to tell John Sanders when he got home.

CHAPTER TWELVE

The next morning, Raider was awakened shortly after daybreak by the smell of fresh bacon frying. He dressed and found his way downstairs to the kitchen. A black woman named Tillie glared at him with big brown eyes.

"You s'posed to eat wid de udder white people."

Raider winked at her. "Aw, I ain't much on white people, Tillie. I feel a lot better when I ain't around 'em."

That made her laugh. "It's 'bout time we got somebody 'round here dat's good for a chuckle or two."

Raider met her gaze. "You sayin' Mrs. Sanders don't like t' laugh?"

Tillie's smile disappeared. "Don't git me started 'bout dat woman. I ain't liable t' shut up once I gits goin'."

"Go ahead an' say your piece," Raider urged. "I'll sit here an' listen as long as you talk."

She waved him off with a dish towel. "Less said de better."

"Aw, you can say more than that, Tillie."

She glared at him. "All I'm sayin' is dat it was a whole lot better 'round here 'fore she came!"

"You don't—"

"Now hush up, you long-legged, black-eyed cowboy. I gotta get your breakfast ready."

She served him eggs, ham, bacon, potatoes, and a loaf of fresh bread. Raider dug in, cleaning two plates before he backed off. She served him coffee when she realized she couldn't get him to eat any more.

Raider was sipping his black coffee when he heard a bell tinkling.

Tillie sighed. "Looks like she wanna have her breakfast in bed dis mornin'. She 'bout de laziest woman I ever knowed."

"She stays out late at night," Raider offered.

Tillie started to make up a tray. "I don' know why he put up wid it. She ain't dat pretty!"

Raider wanted to talk to the woman some more, but Tillie hurried upstairs with breakfast for Ellen Sanders. He got up and strode to the window, peering out at the Green Sands Ranch. It seemed to spread on forever. He knew that there were mountains in the distance, but he could only see vague shadows against the sunny, blue sky.

He also saw dust rising, stirred by an approaching carriage.

John Sanders arrived a few minutes later, accompanied by his man Dennison.

Raider was standing in the parlor when Sanders walked into the fine house. "Mornin'."

Sanders gawked at him. "Why aren't you out looking for Johnny Sonora?"

"I wanted t' talk t' you first," Raider replied.

Sanders hesitated, but then nodded toward an oak door that led to his private study. "All right. Inside. Dennison, bring me a cup of coffee."

The butler nodded. "As you wish, sir."

Raider followed Sanders into the redwood-paneled study. Trophy heads from hunted animals hung on the wall: deer, elk, mountain sheep. A huge desk was covered with papers. Bookshelves supported many volumes behind the desk.

Raider nodded appreciatively. "Looks pretty fair."

Sanders offered him a chair. "Sit down. We don't have time to waste."

Raider took a wooden chair on the other side of the desk.

Sanders sat down behind his stacks of papers. "I do wish you would get started right away, Raider. I am paying you good money, after all."

"Yes, sir, as soon as we get a few things clear."

Sanders frowned. "What are you talking about?"

Raider reached into his vest pocket, taking out the wad of money he had claimed from the ambushers. "Six hundred dollars." He tossed it on the desk. "Good money, ain't it?"

Sanders picked up the cash. "Where did this come from?"

Raider leaned back in the chair. "Took it off three men who tried t' kill me up by the station shack."

"Good God! Is Ellen all right?"

"She's fine," the big man replied. "She don't know a thing 'bout it."

"How'd you pull that off?"

Raider shrugged and smiled. "That's why you're payin' me good money, Sanders. We told her there was a cougar we had t' chase away."

Sanders grunted. "Well, I suppose I should thank you for that. There'll be a bonus in it for you."

"Bonus my ass, Sanders. Somebody wanted me dead enough t' pay nine hundred dollars."

"There's only six here," Sanders challenged.

"I had t' pay the other two t' keep 'em quiet. An' I also had t' give the station man enough t' get rid o' those three bodies."

Sanders shook his head. "He took them into town. I went through Stockton this morning before I came here. The sheriff was asking questions that the station man couldn't answer."

Raider grimaced. "Hmm. Is the station man in any trouble?"

"Not that I know of. But if he's arrested, I'll see to it that he's released. You should probably steer clear of Stockton for now."

"I'm not sure. Those three were hired men, Sanders. The sheriff will probably find posters on 'em. At worst, he'll split the reward money with the station man. Hell, as long as they all get their money, ever'body'll be happy as a sow in slop."

"That's very cynical of you, Raider."

The big man grunted. "I reckon." He didn't know what the hell *cynical* meant. He just hoped it wasn't something bad.

"Look here," Sanders started, "what has all this got to do with the task I've hired you for?"

"Three men tried t' kill me," Raider said. "You explain that first."

Sanders thought about it for a while. "Well, Sonora could have gotten wind that I enlisted you. He might have hired them."

The tall Pinkerton shook his head. "I thought 'bout that. But these weren't the kind o' men that'd run with the California Kid. They were big time regulators. The kind o' men you never hear about. They get in quick, get the job done, an' get out. Too slick for Sonora."

Sanders threw up his hands. "All right. Then they were trying to get you for something you did in the past."

"Mebbe." He looked straight at the older man. "How long you been married t' your wife, Mr. Sanders?"

Anger flashed in the man's gray eyes. "I won't have that kind of talk under my roof, sir!"

Raider leaned forward a little. "I ain't pointin' no fingers, Sanders. Not right away. I'm just sayin' that sometimes trouble begins close t' home. I might be able t' do more good 'round here than if I—"

"I hired you to find Johnny Sonora, to find out why he's using my old name. Now I suggest you get to your task."

Raider sighed. "I don't know, Mr. Sanders. You think somebody wants t' get you an' I think you're right. Somebody sure as hell didn't want me pokin' 'round here. An' those men were hired not too long after you hired me. It looks bad from my angle."

Sanders waved his hands in the air. "Coincidence."

"Mebbe." Raider stared straight at him. "Let me ask you one more thing, Mr. Sanders. Does the name Franklin mean anything to you?"

Sanders's eyes narrowed. "Where did you hear that name?"

"Around. I don't waste no time on the job."

"Franklin Jenkins is one of my opponents in the mayoral race," Sanders replied coldly. "Which means that you are to stay away from him. Do you understand me?"

"What if Jenkins has somethin' t' do with all this?"

Sanders exhaled. "Just go after Sonora, Raider, or I'll have you removed from the case."

Raider considered walking out right then. He didn't like ultimatums from his clients, even if Wagner did say that all agents should be polite in the face of rudeness. He also thought about telling Sanders that his wife had surrendered the night before to a man with the same name as Sanders's political foe. But he decided it would be best to wait a while. If he played his hand now, everyone would know how much he had found out.

"I'm waiting for your answer," Sanders insisted. "Are you going after the California Kid?"

Raider took a deep breath and then let out his answer. "If that's the way you want it, Sanders. Can I get a mount 'round here?"

"Go to the stables, see Luis."

Raider nodded, rose from the chair and started for the door.

"Pinkerton!"

He looked back at Sanders. "Yeah?"

Sanders gestured to the money on his desk, the six hundred dollars that Raider had taken from the ambushers. "Don't you want this?"

"It'll feel more at home with you, Mr. Sanders. I mean, you know how important money can be. Hell, spread it around Stockton if the sheriff makes any noise. I'm sure you'll find somethin' t' do with it."

"But—"

Raider closed the door behind him. He had to get to the stable and find a horse. The big man wasn't quite sure what to do yet. He'd have to think on it a while. Whatever he decided, he would conduct the investigation his own way. Of course, John Sanders didn't have to know about it. Not for a few days, anyway.

Raider was looking over the remuda when he saw Ellen Sanders from the corner of his eye. She was coming straight toward him. Raider fixed his gaze on a huge black stallion that towered above the other animals.

Ellen Sanders came up beside him. "The palomino is a fine mare," she offered. "Pretty, too."

Raider shook his head. "I got some hard ridin' t' do. Look at the chest on that stallion."

She threw a look his way, smiling. "I'll do just that."

Raider chortled a little. "I seen some brazen women in my time, Ellen, but you take the top spot."

"Is it brazen for a woman to know what she wants?"

He turned to face her. "You want Franklin. Don't you, Mrs. Sanders?"

She blushed. "How dare you—"

She started to slap him.

Raider caught her hand. "Is he the one who's runnin' agin' your husband for mayor o' Stockton?"

"You know nothing!"

He leaned against the corral on one arm. "What did you know 'bout that ambush last night?"

She frowned, like she really didn't know. "Ambush?"

Was she that good an actress?

"At the station," Raider offered.

"You said there was a cougar!"

He waved her off. "If you don't wanna talk—"

She stiffened. "Now listen to me. I admit that I'm in love with another man. I won't tell you who it is—"

"If it's your husband's rival, he might be usin' you t' make sure he wins the election."

Tears began to flow from her eyes. "No! Nothing is going to happen between us until after the election."

Raider shook his head. "Somehow I can't b'lieve you. You know, you were awful eager t' be friendly t' me when we first met."

She looked down at the ground. "I thought that John had hired you to spy on me. But now I know that he hasn't."

"How'd you know that?"

She focused her blue eyes on him. "Because you didn't tell him about me sneaking out last night to meet Fr—"

Raider exhaled. "I tried. But he don't wanna hear it."

"This election is the only thing important to him. He won't be sad when I leave him."

"Tell the stable boy to cut the stallion out for me. I'm goin' t' get my gear."

He started away from her.

"Raider."

He looked over his shoulder. "I'm listenin'."

"If somebody is trying to hurt John, please stop them. I don't want anything to happen to him."

A hell of a performance, the big man thought. She was good. Raider just had to convince her husband before they played the final act.

When Raider opened the door to his room, he saw Dennison, the butler, leaning over his gear.

"You find anythin' you like, Dennison?"

The butler flinched when he saw Raider's scowl. "I'm terribly sorry, sir. Mr. Sanders said you were going to be riding out today, so I came up to see if I could give you a hand."

Raider nodded. He figured Dennison was used to going through other people's stuff. It was a habit of his position.

"You can help me drag some o' that stuff down t' the corral," the big man said. "I'm headin' out soon as I can saddle up."

"Very good, sir. Shall I have Tillie prepare some food for you to take along? I'm sure she'd be obliging."

Raider said that some food would be fine.

Dennison started for the door.

"Not so fast," Raider said. "I want you t' answer somethin' for me."

Dennison's face went slack. "If I am able, sir."

"What d' you know 'bout Mrs. Sanders an' this man Jenkins?"

The butler blushed. "I'm not sure I know anything, sir. If you will excuse me—"

Raider stopped him. "Your boss's life may depend on what you know."

Dennison pulled away. "I'm sorry, Mr. Raider, but I cannot betray the confidence of my employer. If you'll excuse me."

Raider shook his head. He had a feeling that Dennison knew more than he was telling. But what the hell could he do? Beat it out of him?

He started to gather up his gear. Maybe he'd find some answers in Stockton. It was the next logical place to start looking.

Raider had only ridden a few miles when he decided that the black stallion had been a good choice. The animal was a little tough to handle at first, but it came around. Raider knew he would have to cover some ground if he wanted to find Johnny Sonora. The California Kid might be able to tell him a few things—if the kid had anything to do with Sanders's trouble.

He slowed the black, enjoying the fine day, taking in the landscape. The rolling countryside was dotted with patches of trees and brush. The sky shone cloudless and blue. It was the kind of day that helped a man clear his head to think about things.

What the hell did he have in this case? Sanders had hired him to find Johnny Sonora, but the real trouble seemed to be closer to home. Mrs. Sanders was fooling around with Sanders's opponent in the election. Oddly enough, though, that tied the whole thing together. Reminding the townfolk of Stockton that Sanders had once been the California Kid was a great way of discrediting him.

But who was behind the return of the California Kid? That knowledge would lead Raider to the truth. Maybe Franklin Jenkins had cooked up the whole thing to smear Sanders. Raider figured he needed to meet the politician, or at least ask around about him. He had to steer clear of the politics, though. The agency would never approve of a Pinkerton making a difference in an election.

His task was simple; find out about the California Kid and report it to his employer. Nothing more or less. He'd dig up the information Sanders wanted and then dismiss himself from the case.

Of course, he'd go at it his own way. Nobody was going to tell the big man from Arkansas how to conduct an investigation. First stop, Franklin Jenkins in Stockton.

He spurred the stallion into a gallop, heading toward town.

Fate really didn't care which direction you were taking. Sometimes the cards just fell in a certain way and you had to play them. Raider was dealt a strange hand when he rode into Stockton. It wasn't completely bad, however. He found Franklin Jenkins right away.

There was a banner drawn across the neat little main street of Stockton. The banner declared that there were "Big Speeches Today." As Raider rode under the billowing placard that spanned the thoroughfare, he saw the crowd gathered in front of the platform.

A man stood on the platform, addressing the people who had gathered before him. Raider tied the black at a hitching post and strode toward the spectacle. He hung on the back edge of the throng, watching the man as he gestured to the townsfolk.

"I'm for Stockton," he told them. "For you! The people. And if you elect me mayor, I won't let you down!"

They applauded, although Raider figured he had heard better in his day. Still, he had to admit that the man inspired an almost instantaneous trust. He was handsome with clear brown eyes and a thick head of hair. About Raider's age, not as tall, but he had strong, broad shoulders. Dressed in a neat suit, like most politicians.

"Stockton is growing," the orator extolled, "and I want us all to grow with it. Are you with me?"

Some of them applauded, but others didn't seem as convinced.

"I'm for Sanders!" someone cried.

The man on the platform ignored the heckler. "One day California will be the most prosperous state in this union. And Stockton will be the most prosperous town in California, or my name is not Benjamin Franklin Jenkins!"

Raider flinched.

"You tell 'em, Franklin!"

"I'm with you, Jenkins!"

The man on the platform was Ellen Sanders's boyfriend. Raider should have figured it out right away. Somehow he hadn't connected the honest-faced man with the midnight rendezvous at Green Sands Ranch. Jenkins appeared to be younger than Mrs. Sanders, although his looks could have been deceiving. He seemed so damned honest!

"I care about each and every citizen of this community," he went on. "I grew up here. I went to school here. I worked as a teacher and I studied law in the office above my father's store. Now, I don't want to belittle my opponents in this race. I just want to say that I'm going to keep on living in Stockton whether I win the election or not. I'm one of you!"

They agreed that he was.

"And we're together all the way."

They cheered him.

Raider tipped back his Stetson, watching Jenkins. The politician really wasn't saying much, but the way he said it was convincing. Even the ones who had been against him were taken in.

Was Jenkins the kind to let a woman lead him around by the nose? Mrs. Sanders probably knew enough tricks to please any man, but Raider had to wonder if she was worth risking an election. How would it look to the townsfolk if their hero was topping his opponent's wife?

Jenkins went on, making all of the same promises that politicians made. Raider watched the crowd, wondering how the citizens of Stockton would react when he started asking around about their favorite son.

When Jenkins finished his speech, he walked among his audience, shaking hands and kissing babies. Eventually the campaigner made it to the back of the crowd where Raider stood. He came toe to toe with the big man, extending his hand. His handshake was firm and sure.

"You from Stockton?" he asked Raider.

"Er, no, but I hope t' be someday."

Jenkins smiled. "You couldn't pick a better place to live, sir."

He walked on, flanked by his admirers.

Another speaker ascended the platform but the voters were following Jenkins down the street. Probably having a party for them. Raider looked toward the new speaker. He wondered why Sanders was absent from the gathering. Maybe he had spoken earlier in the day. Sanders had been in Stockton that morning. He had probably given his speech then. Raider couldn't blame him for not wanting to compete head-on with Jenkins.

Suddenly the big man felt confused. Why the hell would Jenkins engineer a plot to discredit Sanders when he seemed to be a shoo-in for mayor? If anything, it seemed like Sanders would be the one to play dirty. Maybe he was just reading the whole thing wrong.

The big Pinkerton wasn't really sure what to do next. He considered staying in Stockton to ask about Franklin Jenkins, but something told him that was the wrong thing to do. He figured the citizens wouldn't be eager to say bad things about Jenkins. They might even try to cause trouble for Raider.

So the only thing left to do was go after Johnny Sonora, the job he had been hired for in the first place. He didn't have to debate with himself for very long. When he saw the sheriff striding toward him, with his badge glistening in the sunlight, Raider untied the stallion and swung into the saddle. He headed north, away from Stockton, hoping that he was doing the right thing.

Raider had never remembered liking California, but the northern ranges of the state captured his fancy. The air was clear, the sky blue, the breeze cool. He bore on with the stallion under him, heading due north. He wondered if he would have to go all the way back to Yreka to pick up the trail of the California Kid.

There was no word of Johnny Sonora in Roseville or Colusa. The kid hadn't come this far south. Raider rested for a night in Colusa, sleeping in the loft of a farmer. The man also fed him, a meal that Raider tried to pay a dollar for, but the farmer wouldn't take the money.

Raider went on the next morning, plodding toward Yreka. What if the kid had run back into Oregon? A trail away from Stockton would put an end to Sanders's suspicions that somebody was trying to discredit him by bringing Johnny Sonora out of his past.

Then again, a trail south might mean just the opposite. Maybe somebody really was trying to get Sanders. A former gunslinger might have enemies that he had forgotten about.

Raider held steady, making his way through the valleys between the wooded slopes. Nobody had heard of Johnny Sonora in Willows. In Hamilton City somebody had heard of the California Kid, but the man wasn't sure if the kid was operating in this part of the state.

The big man slept on the ground that night, slapping a few mosquitoes that hovered around his face.

He rode on the next day, almost sure that he was wasting his time. At least until he reached Red Bluff. There, on the porch of the general store, a man told an eyewitness account of a blond boy with a fast gun. The man had seen him cut down another man in a fair fight, over in Shingletown. Fastest draw the man had ever seen.

Raider asked if the blond boy had a name.

The storyteller wasn't sure about his real name, but he had heard that the boy was called the California Kid.

Johnny Sonora wasn't very clever about hiding his tracks.

The saloonkeeper in Shingletown recounted the gunfight for Raider, adding a few details, mainly that the kid had provoked the confrontation. Of course, the dead man had drawn first. The kid was just faster.

According to the barman, the kid said he was heading south.

Raider finished his whiskey and rode on.

Johnny Sonora had been rude to a storekeeper in Tobin. A justice of the peace had asked him, politely, to leave Butte City. Sonora was traveling alone as far as the justice could see.

Raider thanked him and mounted up again. Sonora had taken a southeastern trail from Yreka, but now he was winding down toward Sacramento. Was he making for Stockton and John Sanders?

Raider just missed him in Oroville. He had backtracked for almost a week. A bank teller in Oroville told him how Sonora had cashed five twenty-dollar gold pieces for banknotes and smaller coins. He had also been rude to the teller.

Halfway between Oroville and Yuba City, Raider got a description of a man who looked exactly like Johnny Sonora. He had passed a tinker just a couple of hours earlier. Said he was making for Yuba City on a tall buckskin.

Closer and closer, the big man thought. He just hoped he could find Sonora before the kid decided to make real trouble.

CHAPTER THIRTEEN

There wasn't much to Yuba City. Raider almost rode past the few brown buildings that sat on the horizon like a bug on a mule's back. He turned the stallion toward the dingy shapes, riding slowly into town.

He kept his eyes open, hoping to see a tall buckskin tied to one of the hitching posts. Sure enough, the animal had been tethered in front of a small adobe hut that probably served as the town's cantina. Raider dismounted and tied the stallion next to the buckskin.

The big man hesitated at the doorway, patting the butt of his Colt with his gun hand. He reminded himself that he was not chasing an outlaw, but just trying to find someone. Someone who was really fast with a pistol. Raider had some doubts as to his ability to take Sonora in a gunfight. Maybe he wouldn't have to find out the hard way.

He took a deep breath and pushed into the cantina.

It was dark inside. He had to wait for his black eyes to focus in the shadows. His head turned, scanning the denizens of the crude saloon. He didn't see any blond-haired kids with pistols hanging low on their hips. Where the hell had Sonora gone?

Best just to sit for a while. He found his way to a table. An

101

ugly woman asked what he wanted. Raider ordered a tequila, which was warm and homemade. He didn't ask the woman about Sonora. She might warn the kid if she knew somebody was looking for him.

When the tequila started his head spinning, Raider put down the wooden cup. He wanted his senses to be clear, in case the California Kid showed his face. Maybe Sonora was in back. Maybe the cantina had a gambling room or a couple of whores.

Raider was on the verge of an inquiry when the blond kid came in from a back door. Johnny Sonora buttoned the last button on his fly. He stopped and looked around the room, focusing finally on Raider. The big man nodded.

Sonora started for the door.

Raider rose from the chair, thinking that it was going to be tough to get any answers out of the kid.

But then somebody called Sonora's name and the cantina was filled with the explosive sound of gunfire.

"Sonora!"

The kid turned to face the dark man who had called his name.

Raider froze, his hand hovering over his Colt.

"Sonora, you son of a bitch. You ran out on us. Now you got to pay for what you did."

Sonora squinted at the man's face. "Kilmer?"

"You're damned right."

Kilmer's hands were out to his sides. He wore an old army Colt in a Mexican holster. Not the kind of man who could be talked out of drawing.

Sonora had a thin smile on his face. His hand was hanging low over a Peacemaker. It was almost like he wanted a fight.

"You left us hangin' high and dry, Sonora."

"I ain't much on robbin' banks, Kilmer. I told you that before I started to ride with you."

Was Raider hearing right? The California Kid didn't want to be a bank robber. What the hell was going on?

Kilmer hit himself in the chest. "I call the shots in my gang. And you run out. Got two of my men killed."

"Watch those hands," Sonora said. "You wouldn't do right to pull on me, Kilmer. You know you're not fast enough."

Kilmer licked his lips. "I got no choice, Sonora."

The kid's body tensed. "Your move, Kilmer. You know I never draw on a man less'n he draws first."

Raider didn't believe what he had heard. Same as in Yreka. The kid had let those men go for their guns before he drew. At least he was honest in that way. Or just confident in his gun skill.

Sonora nodded toward the front door. "I'm givin' you one more chance to clear out of here, Kilmer. Either back off or go for your iron."

The other drinkers in the cantina started to scatter, like they finally believed the gunfight was going to happen.

Raider had to wonder himself. The man called Kilmer wore a gleam of doubt in his eyes. Like he had seen the kid draw before.

"Do or die, Kilmer," Sonora challenged.

Kilmer couldn't back off. His mouth had started the fire and now his ass had to put it out. He figured to pay with his life by going for his gun.

Kilmer was fast.

But Sonora was faster. Raider couldn't be sure that he had seen the kid's gun hand actually moving. The Colt just seemed to appear in his grip, barking fire, sending a single shot into the man's chest.

Kilmer staggered forward, his gun falling from his hand. He went down face first on the floor, twitching as the life flowed out of him. Everybody held still for a moment. Sonora finally took a step toward the body.

"He drew first," the kid said, smiling. He turned to Raider, who had his hand on his Colt. The kid was going to ask him if he wanted to fight.

But Raider was already lifting his gun from the holster. "Sonora, look out!"

The kid dived quickly to his right.

Raider fired twice into the shadows.

Sonora came up on one knee, pointing his pistol at the big man. "You're gonna get it now, asshole."

Raider waved his Colt at the other side of the room. "Take a look at that afore you pull the trigger."

A man staggered from the shadows. He held a shotgun in his hand. He dropped the scattergun and clutched his chest. Both of Raider's bullets had hit him in the heart. Blood poured between his fingers. He opened his mouth but nothing came out. His body thumped to the floor.

Raider holstered up and strode toward the dead man. He turned him over and looked down at his face. Sonora stepped beside Raider, still holding his .45 with the hammer thumbed back.

"You know him?" Raider asked.

The California Kid nodded. "He's one of Kilmer's men."

Raider tipped back his Stetson. "Seen him in the dark there. He was gettin' ready t' give you both barrels in the shoulder blades. Backin' up his boss, I reckon."

Sonora stepped away, lowering the pistol. "You called my name!"

Raider shrugged. "So?"

"You know me?"

"I saw you kill two men in Yreka," Raider said. "You were pretty fast. They pulled on you as I recall."

The California Kid lowered the weapon. "Yeah, seems I remember you, too. You drew but you stayed calm. Didn't try to shoot me."

"Never like t' get involved with another man's fight."

Sonora holstered up and then gestured to the second dead man. "You took care of that one pretty fast."

"Never cotton t' backshootin' neither."

Sonora smiled. "Reckon I owe you."

"Buy me a tequila an' we'll call it square."

The kid nodded. He turned to the cantina man, who seemed to be unfazed by the shooting. "How much to bury 'em, Pedro?"

"Twenty dollars."

"Okay. And bring us a bottle of the best whiskey you got." He looked at Raider. "That okay with you, big man?"

"Call me Ray."

As they sat down at a crude table, Raider was surprised at how much he had in common with the California Kid.

The whiskey was homemade, but it was a hell of a lot better than the tequila. The kid seemed ready to tie one on. He matched Raider shot for shot. Even ordered some warm beer to wash down the hooch.

Raider eyed the kid, wondering if he could get him to talk. "How come that dead one was after you, Sonora?"

The kid shrugged. "I made the mistake of ridin' with him and his boys for a while. You know how it is. You're goin' some-place and you fall in with the wrong sort."

"Wrong how?"

"Kilmer thought he wanted to rob some bank," Sonora replied. "That's what you saw in Yreka. I was supposed to split off with those ones I killed. But when I found out what they was up to, well, I just couldn't go along with it. When I told them I wasn't robbin' any banks, they thought I wanted a bigger share. And then—well, you saw the rest."

Raider squinted at the kid. "You know, Sonora, you got some-thin' of a reputation in these parts."

The kid glanced sideways at him. "How's that?"

Raider leaned forward, grabbing the bottle. "Well," he said, pouring himself another shot, "some say you're called the California Kid."

Sonora smiled. "Is that so?"

"I reckon. Is it true?"

"Why you askin'?"

Raider knocked back a shot of the hooch. "Hell, it don't make much difference to me. I killed a couple o' men who called their-selves by the same name. I was just wonderin' if you was re-lated?"

Sonora chortled. "No, 'fraid not."

Raider looked straight at him. "There's also a man, a long time ago, who was called by that name. One of the old-time gunfighters, afore the war. You know anythin' 'bout that?"

"Can't say as I do," Sonora replied with a grin. "Why you so innersted? You the law or somethin'?"

Raider leaned back in the chair, showing the palms of his hands. "Hey, it ain't no never mind. I just heard the name afore."

Sonora nodded. "I seen you with that gun there, Ray. You ain't so slow yourself. Got off two in a hurry. You a gunfighter?"

The big man forced a laugh. "Well, I don't look for trouble, but it always seems t' find me."

Sonora shook his head. "You know, I'm the same way. I don't know what it is. You kill a few people and you never hear the end of it. Even if they're tryin' to kill you. Why—"

He broke off. The front door had opened. The kid's eyes grew wide, like he expected the law. Instead, a skinny man with a sombrero slid into the cantina. He hesitated, staring into the shadows, stopping when his eyes fell on Sonora.

The California Kid sighed. "There it is, Ray."

Raider knew what Sonora was talking about. The local punk. A green kid who had practiced his quick draw on green glass bottles.

"You the California Kid?" the skinny man asked.

"I won't kill you if you go back out that door," Sonora offered.

But the skinny man wasn't even going to give him a chance to stand up. He went for his sidearm. Raider didn't think Sonora had a prayer, but the Colt seemed to appear in the kid's hand, erupting only once, sending the man in the sombrero to his reward.

The cantina man shook an angry finger at the kid. "That's goin' to cost you another five!"

"I'm good for it," Sonora replied, holstering his weapon.

Raider whistled. "You're as fast as they say."

"There's always somebody faster," the kid replied. "The town punk there can tell you that. There's always one. Hell, I wish I didn't have a rep. It could make things a whole lot easier."

Raider considered telling him about the way the first California Kid had shaken his history to become an outstanding citizen. But Raider decided against it. If the big man volunteered too much information, the kid might figure out that Raider was up to something. He still wasn't sure about Johnny Sonora. Maybe the kid did have something in mind for John Sanders.

"Got to go shake the dew from my lily," Sonora said. "Help yourself to the whiskey."

Raider nodded, pouring himself another shot. The booze didn't seem to have much effect on the kid. Raider considered following Sonora to the outhouse, but he didn't want to appear too eager to keep a watch on the kid. If Sonora didn't come back into the cantina, Raider could follow him again by picking up his trail.

He sat there, wondering what the hell was going on. Except for killing people, Johnny Sonora seemed like a pretty good hombre. Quick to buy a drink, unwanting of his reputation, friendlier than most gunfighters. Raider liked him in a strange sort of way. Best not to be taken in until he had the whole truth about him.

Sonora came back in and sat at the table. "Sure been good

talkin' to you, Ray. Hell, sometimes I think you're the only one in this territory who ain't tryin' to kill me."

"Never have been one t' fight with any man who'd buy me a drink."

The kid looked straight at him. "What's your line o' work?"

Raider grimaced. "Line o' work?"

"You must do somethin' to make a livin'."

Raider laughed. "You mean like a job?"

"Somethin' like that."

"Only job I got is stayin' away from work," Raider replied. "There's enough things a man can do t' get money without hard work."

The kid frowned at him. "Look here, Ray. I told you I ain't one to break the law."

Raider waved him off, laughing. "Aw, hell, boy, I ain't talkin' 'bout stealin' or killin'. You know what I mean when I say that. Ain't you never shot deer an' then sold the meat an' hides? Or panned for gold?"

"Yeah, I reckon. You ever take to bounty huntin'?"

Raider shook his head. "Ain't much t' gettin' paid for another man's hide, Sonora. How 'bout you?"

"I killed a man in Hunters Falls once. The sheriff gave me fifty dollars 'cause the man was wanted."

"That ain't the same as bounty huntin'."

"I reckon not."

They sat there, drinking for a while. Johnny Sonora took out a harmonica and played a few songs that got everybody to tapping their feet. He stopped playing when the sheriff walked in.

"Hear you had some trouble," the sheriff said to the cantina owner.

The man pointed at Johnny Sonora.

The California Kid tensed.

Raider told him to stay still. "You said you don't want no trouble, Sonora. So let me do the talkin'."

The sheriff walked toward them. "Are you the boys who were gunfightin'?"

Raider grinned at him. "Depends on what you call gunfightin', sheriff. We were just protectin' ourselves. Ask anybody who saw it."

Everybody, including the cantina man, backed up Raider's claim.

"They all drew first."

"That's right, these two was in the right."

The sheriff sighed. "Well, I'll have to let it stand. But it might be a good idea if you boys ride on after you finish your liquor."

Johnny Sonora smiled at the law. "Sure as shit, sheriff. My compañero and me, we're just leavin'. Plan to head on to Sacramento. If that's all right with you."

Raider could tell the sheriff didn't like the kid's smart-ass attitude, but the lawman let it ride. "Just get gone, before there's more trouble."

He turned and left the cantina.

"I hate lawmen," the kid said. "And they don't seem to like me neither."

Raider went along with him. "Can't say as I like 'em neither. Hey, that true what you said, 'bout ridin' t' Sacramento?"

The kid nodded. "Didn't mean to put you on the spot, but you're welcome to ride along."

Raider said that was all right with him. Now he could keep an eye on the kid firsthand. Of course, he'd play it careful. Johnny Sonora was too fast with his gun. Raider still wasn't sure he could take him in a fair fight. And he sure as hell hoped he never had to find out.

"Sacramento."

Raider eased the stallion to a halt next to Sonora's buckskin. They were on a small ridge that looked down on the capital of California. The ride had been uneventful. Sonora wasn't a bad traveling partner. Kept his mouth shut and knew where to stop to find whiskey.

The big man from Arkansas nodded toward town. "This the last stop on the trail?"

Sonora ignored the question. "You know, Ray, you look like a man who could stand to have his beard trimmed." He urged the buckskin into a walk.

Raider fell in beside him. "Yeah, I reckon I could use a bath an' a shave at that."

The kid laughed. "That ain't the kind of beard I'm talkin' about."

"Come again?"

The kid took a deep breath. "Let's just say that I know a house outside the town line. You probably know the kind of place I'm talkin' about. Ladies. Lots of ladies."

Raider smiled. "Ladies who don't get up early for breakfast."

"You got it, partner."

"We goin' there right now?" Raider asked.

"I am," Sonora replied. "You're welcome to come if you want to."

He spurred the buckskin into a lope.

Raider followed on the stallion, hoping it wasn't a trap.

Johnny Sonora hadn't been lying about the Sacramento whorehouse. It was the sort of establishment that Raider could appreciate. A big, bright, two-story house painted yellow and white. Curtains in the windows, stable out back, a man to take your horse when you rode up.

They reached the cathouse around five in the afternoon. The girls weren't ready yet, but a round, dark-haired woman came to meet them. She smiled when she saw the kid.

"Bobby," she said, "it's been a long time."

Sonora kissed her on the cheek. "Hello, Lisa. This is my pard, Ray. Think we could get a few drinks and some grub before the evenin' starts?"

She winked at him. "Anything for you, Bobby. Follow me."

She turned down a long hallway, heading for a kitchen.

Raider looked at Sonora. "She's got you confused with somebody else."

"How's that?" the kid replied.

"Callin' you Bobby. That ain't your name."

Sonora grinned at him. "You always give your proper name when you're whorin', big man?"

Raider figured the kid had a point. Unless there was more to it and Sonora was hiding something. Best just to stay with the matters at hand, try to pretend he was just enjoying himself.

In the large kitchen at the back of the house, Lisa fixed them meat and potatoes. After eating rabbit for a dog's age, Raider was ready for some good beef. He finished his dinner and turned his attention to the bottle of whiskey that Lisa had put on the table.

"She's a good woman," Sonora offered. "Hell, I'd marry her if I was the marryin' kind."

Raider sipped the whiskey from a shot glass. "Yeah, I know what you mean. Thanks for showin' me this place, Johnny. I don't spend much time in California, but I'm still s'prised that this one slipped by me."

"Call me Bobby while we're here."

Raider nodded. "Sure 'nuff."

Lisa floated back into the room, all perfumed and powdered in her flowing silk robes. "You boys get enough to eat?" She put her hands on Sonora's shoulders, squeezing gently.

The kid smiled up at her. "Yeah, we're ready for some real fun now, Lisa. How long before you're open for business?"

"Not long. You boys just stay here until I say so."

Raider nodded. "Thanks, ma'am."

"Oooh, he's so polite," Lisa replied. "Say, cowboy, what kind of girls do you like?"

"I usually like 'em alive," Raider replied. "After that, I ain't too picky 'bout it."

"Comin' right up," she said, leaving them again.

"Good ol' girl," Raider offered.

Sonora was looking sideways at the big man.

"Somethin' on your mind, Joh—I mean, Bobby?"

The kid exhaled, shaking his head. "I was just thinkin' that you're as fast with a gun as I am."

Raider squinted at him. "How come you to think like that?"

Sonora shrugged. "Well, it'd just be a real shame if we was to fight. Yeah, a real shame." He looked at Raider like he was waiting for a reply.

The tall Pinkerton from Arkansas had a blank expression on his face. "Yeah," he said in a low voice. "That'd be a real shame."

The dark-haired girl lay back on the featherbed with her big breasts spilling to both sides. Sonora had arranged for them to stay all night at the cathouse. Raider had even gotten to choose the girl who would spend the night with him. She was Mexican, although she spoke crystal-clear English.

"Hey, cowboy, you gonna spend the whole night at that window?"

Raider stood at the casement, still fully clothed. He was watching the stable in the back, wondering if Sonora was going to run out on him. Something just didn't feel right. Raider couldn't put his finger on it exactly. The kid just seemed too calm and collected.

"Cowboy! Are you listenin' to me?"

Raider glanced back at her, feeling the sudden tightness in his jeans. "Wanna make sure they took good care o' my mount," he said.

"You came in with Bobby, right?"

Raider nodded.

"It's okay," the girl replied. "You'll get the best. From the stable. From me. Come to bed."

Raider didn't go right away, so she climbed out, sliding next to him. Her dark skin was flawless. Big brown eyes. What else could he do? If he didn't follow through, word might get back to Sonora and make him suspicious.

Her hands moved down his stomach to his crotch. "Damn," she said when she felt his prick. "You're gettin' into bed with me right now!"

She stripped him of his clothes in a couple of minutes. Raider was hard and ready. Too many days in the saddle had left him vulnerable to her smooth hands and nimble fingers. She made him lie back on the bed.

"God, it's so big. Here, let me do it."

She stroked him up and down, making funny noises through her lips.

"Lie down," Raider said finally.

"No," the girl replied, "I'm gonna be on top."

She straddled him, guiding his massive prickhead to the open folds of her dark cunt. In one motion, she swallowed him into her, bouncing up and down on his length. Raider cupped her flouncing breasts, rubbing the nipples with his palms.

"Don't shoot yet," she told him.

Raider reached for her backside, grabbing the round cheeks of her big ass. "My turn to be on top now."

He rolled her over without missing a beat. She raised her legs to the ceiling and begged him to do it hard. As hard as he could. Deep. All the way. Like she never had it so good.

Raider felt his release rising. He buried his cock inside her, exploding, evoking deep cries from her throat. Her body shook and she wrapped him in arms and legs to keep him inside.

"More," she said. "I can make you hard again."

He tried to roll off her.

"No," she protested. "Don't take it out. Leave it in."

Raider didn't want Sonora to leave without him, but the woman was persistent. She kept him busy until his eyes were closed. He slept for a long time, waking next to her the following morning.

He climbed out of bed and looked toward the stable. Everything seemed calm enough. Raider dressed quickly and hurried downstairs to the kitchen.

Lisa was making coffee. "You want a cup of the hot stuff, cowboy?"

Raider smiled at her. "Think I'll wait for my pard to come down."

"Bobby? He's already gone. Rode out about dawn."

Raider felt the churning in his stomach. "Did he say where he was goin'?"

"Said to look him up if you ever got to Stockton. Hey, cowboy, what about your coffee?"

But the big man from Arkansas was already halfway to the stable.

CHAPTER FOURTEEN

Raider rode hard, reaching Stockton by late afternoon. He walked the stallion down the main avenue, watching for the kid's buckskin. It wasn't tied by the sheriff's office. Raider had to wonder if the local authorities had accepted the station man's story about the three dead men that had been killed in the ambush. Maybe the whole thing had blown over by now.

He reined up when he saw the buckskin tied in front of the saloon. The lathered animal was standing on one hindquarter. Had it taken up lame?

Raider stabled his mount and strode quickly to the saloon. He went through the swinging doors, marching straight for the bar. He ordered a whiskey, pretending not to notice Johnny Sonora at the other end of the bar.

"Hey, big man. Down here."

Raider heard the kid's voice. He turned toward the other end of the bar, breaking into a smile when he saw Sonora. He told the bartender to give him a bottle to share with his friend.

Sonora didn't offer to shake hands. "You followin' me, Ray?"

"Can't say that I am."

"Didn't know you was headin' to Stockton," Sonora said.

Raider shrugged. "Mebbe find some work in these parts. I—"

There was a commotion at the entrance of the barroom. Raider and the kid turned to watch. A man came through the double doors, raising his hands. It was Franklin Jenkins, candidate for mayor.

"Friends!" he clamored. "I'm Franklin Jenkins and I want you to vote for me for mayor next week. Cast your ballot at the courthouse. And if you don't vote for me, well, I want to buy you a drink anyway!"

That made everybody cheer.

Jenkins went back into the street, canvassing from door to door.

Sonora shook his head. "I ain't takin' a free drink from no stump-thumper. Throw my drink in the spitoon."

Raider eyed the kid, wondering if it was an act. If Sonora didn't know Franklin Jenkins, then that meant he hadn't been hired by the politician. Somebody else might have enlisted the kid to take Sanders's old name to discredit him. But Sonora still wasn't much of an outlaw, even if he had a knack for killing people.

The big man figured there was only one way to find out the truth. "Hey, Sonora, you ridin' on after this?"

Sonora smiled, refilling his glass from the bottle. "Well, now, Ray, it seems to me that Stockton is the kind of place where a man might find his fortune. You know what I mean?"

Raider chortled. "Mebbe. That stump-thumper seems to have done all right for hisself."

Sonora grimaced. "Aw, that kind always finds a tit to suck on. No, I'm talkin' about somethin' big."

Raider felt it coming. The confession. He had ridden with Sonora long enough for the kid to trust him. Now Sonora was going to share some secret and it might just be the key to the truth.

"Yeah, Ray, I'm gonna be in the chips pretty soon. You see—"

Raider was leaning forward, eager to hear him out. But fate dealt that fifth card to bust the flush, to ruin the straight. Hell, it was probably overdue anyway. He had been too lucky of late.

Sonora lowered his head. "Shit."

"What is it?" Raider asked.

The kid gestured to the door. "Look who's here."

Raider turned, expecting to see a punk with a gun. Instead,

the sheriff stood there with his hands on his hips. He was scanning the crowd, looking for somebody in particular.

Sonora shook his head. "He's gonna talk to me."

"You can't be sure 'bout that," Raider said. "He might be lookin' for anybody. Hell, you just rode into town."

"I always get it," the kid went on. "Lawmen just naturally tell me to move on. It always happens this way."

Raider kept his eye on the sheriff. "Naw, it—"

The lawman started straight for them. Maybe Sonora was right. His reputation had spread all over. No constable wanted the California Kid in his jurisdiction. Better to ask him to leave; that way they never had to face the kid in a showdown. It was a good way for a sheriff to finish out his elected term.

"Is he comin'?" Sonora asked.

Raider nodded. "He's probably up for reelection too. Just stay calm. He's prob'ly got deputies t' back him up."

"I ain't takin' any shit off a lawman, Ray."

"Hold still, kid. Let's see what he has t' say."

The lawman stopped right behind them and introduced himself. "I'm Sheriff Calderwood," he said. "I want to talk to you."

Sonora gawked at him. "I ain't got a damn thing to say to you, sheriff. Less'n you want to charge me with somethin'."

The lawman glanced sideways at Sonora. "You ain't the one I want to talk to, stranger. It's the big man here that I come to see."

Raider squinted at the sheriff. "Me?"

"Your name Raider?"

"Well, sometimes I go by that. But you can call me Ray."

The sheriff tipped back his Stetson. "Ray, huh? You're the Pinkerton."

Raider felt his gut turning over.

The kid backed away from the bar. "Whoa."

"I ain't no Pinkerton," Raider said, glaring at the lawman. "Who told you I was?"

"It's been spreadin' around," the sheriff replied. "Word is that John Sanders hired you for bodyguardin'."

Johnny Sonora smiled at the big man from Arkansas. "So long, Ray. I gotta be goin'."

"Hey, kid, this lawman ain't—"

Sonora raised his hand. "Adios, amigo."

"Aw, don't b'lieve—"

The smile disappeared from the kid's face. "You stay on your side and I'll stay on my side, Ray."

"You got it all wrong, Johnny, I ain't—"

"You been a friend to me," Sonora said. "Let's leave it that way. I don't want to have to face you, Ray. And you don't want to face me."

"Ain't gonna be no fightin'," Raider offered.

"There sure ain't." The kid started for the door. "So long, Ray. It's been good to know you."

He walked through the swinging doors and mounted the buckskin.

Raider heard him ride away.

"What's wrong with him?" the sheriff asked.

Raider glared at the lawman again. "Thanks, sheriff. You just ruint a whole lotta good work."

"I don't understand."

"No, I reckon you don't. What the hell d' you wanna see me 'bout anyway?"

The sheriff exhaled. "Let's go to my office and talk about it there."

"You arrestin' me?" Raider asked.

"No, but I want to talk to you about those three men who were killed out at the stage stop."

"Aw right. Hell, let's make it quick."

Raider figured it was better to talk in private anyway, even if the whole damned town already seemed to know his business.

The sheriff paced back and forth in front of a big map that showed the layout of Stockton and the surrounding territory. Raider studied the map, wondering where the hell Johnny Sonora had gone. The kid had said that he intended to stay in the area to seek his fortune. What the hell had he meant by that?

"What do you know about those three men who were killed out by the stage stop?" the lawman asked him.

Raider shrugged. "That's a funny place for a stop, ain't it. Why'd they stick it out there anyway?"

"Runs on to Manteca," the sheriff replied. "Comes back through the stop for horses again and then swings back into town. There's no railroad from here to Manteca. That's why they need the stage."

Raider nodded appreciatively. "Makes sense."

The sheriff stared straight at him. "You still ain't answered my question, Pinkerton."

"How's that?"

"Do you know anything about those three men who were killed out there?"

Raider leaned back in the wooden chair, stretching out his legs. "Sheriff, are you arrestin' me?"

"No."

"Then why are you askin' me all these questions?"

The sheriff sighed. "Well, Pete just don't seem like the kind to shoot three men like that."

"Like what?"

"I ain't sure," the lawman replied. "They were hired guns. Could tell it by looking at them. Don't seem like old Pete could have killed all three of them without gettin' hurt."

Raider looked back at the sheriff. "Can I ask you somethin'?"

"Okay. Even if you ain't answerin' me."

"Were those men wanted? Prices on their head?"

The sheriff nodded. "I gave the reward to Pete. The posters stated dead or alive."

Raider sat up straight. "Sheriff, I killed those three men at the stage stop. They were tryin' t' ambush the coach. When we started t' pull up, the driver noticed the lights weren't on in the station house. So I set a little trap an' caught all three of 'em." He didn't figure he would say that the driver had shot one of the men. He didn't want to get the driver in trouble.

The sheriff rubbed his chin. "Well, thanks for tellin' the truth."

"Am I free t' go?"

"Not just yet. I wanna know why you're workin' for John Sanders."

Raider shook his head. "That's b'tween me an' Sanders," he replied. "If you wanna know why I'm workin' for him, ask the man hisself."

"This ain't got nothin' to do with the election, has it?"

"I ain't sure, sheriff. I can give you my word that I won't do anythin' t' mess up the election. Hell, my job might already be over. I ain't sure 'bout that neither."

"I could lock you up until you tell me," the lawman offered.

Raider shrugged, smiling. "Mebbe. But you owe me, sheriff. You told that kid I was a Pinkerton. I didn't want him t' know."

"What's he got to do with all this?"

"I can't tell you, sheriff. I just can't tell you."

The lawman paced again, thinking. Raider figured he wouldn't be locked up. Nobody was going to press the issue of the three dead men. Hell, if anything, it might help Sanders if the voters found out that his hired Pinkerton had killed three desperados.

Sheriff Calderwood finally sat down behind his desk. "You think I'm gonna have any trouble with that kid?"

"I don't know, sheriff. If you have to face him, make sure you got a couple o' men with rifles. Hell, that might not be enough."

The lawman frowned. "Yeah? He's that fast?"

"You don't even see his hand move."

"How fast are you?"

"Fast enough," the big man replied. "Both of us might wind up dead if I was to pull on the kid."

Calderwood slapped the top of his desk. "Damn it, why did all of this have to blow in right around election time?"

"Hell, that's the kind of thing trouble likes best. It don't never come when it's peaceful or when it'll be easy to get rid of. It always blows in the storm when you ain't ready for it."

The sheriff reached into his desk for a bottle of whiskey. "You want a snort, Pinkerton?"

Raider declined.

Calderwood took a long pull from the bottle and then put it back in the desk drawer. "I got to make a decision here."

"How's that, sheriff?"

"Well, this is how it shapes up for me. Sanders hired you. You killed the three men at the station, even though I gave Pete the reward—"

"I didn't want no reward—"

"—but there's nothin' wrong there. I can turn my head, since they was all wanted men. But I ain't sure I can turn my head with you operatin' in my town. On the other hand, if I make trouble for you and Sanders gets elected mayor, I could have a problem there."

Raider chortled a little. "Yeah, it does seem a mite sticky."

The sheriff pointed a finger at him. "If I let you go, will you call me at the first sign of trouble?"

Raider assured him that he would.

"You think you can solve this, Pinkerton? Whatever you're onto?"

"Sheriff, I been stompin' 'round in shit for a couple o' weeks an' I don't have nothin' t' show for it. Like I said afore, I might already be finished. But if things get deep, I'll holler t' you from the middle o' the creek. Is that a deal?"

"Deal. Now get on out of here."

Raider didn't linger. He pushed outside, where he saw a crowd gathering. He wondered if Franklin Jenkins was having another rally. He walked toward the crowd, searching for the center of attention.

"Hey," somebody called, "Sanders is buyin' drinks for ever'body. Come on, 'fore the whiskey runs dry."

Raider followed them, hoping to talk to his boss. He fought his way into the saloon, cutting a path until he was face to face with Sanders. The old gent nodded, gazing expectantly at Raider.

"I need t' talk t' you, sir!" the big man said.

"Later, at the ranch."

Raider nodded and got the hell out of the noisy barroom. Best to let Sanders have his day. In the meantime, he could look for Johnny Sonora—if the California Kid was still in Stockton.

Raider couldn't find Johnny Sonora anywhere. Of course, that didn't mean that he had fled the area, even if he was avoiding Raider. And even if he had run out pretty quickly when he found out Raider was a Pinkerton, that didn't necessarily mean the kid was up to something. Sonora had a distrust of anyone associated with the law. And like it or not, Raider had to admit that he was always on the side of justice.

He searched until late in the evening, hoping he might see Sonora at one of the saloons. The local cathouse also turned up empty. The kid was definitely laying low.

When Raider went back to the stable to get his horse, he asked the livery man if Sonora had been around. The man said that he had seen a blond man ride out on a buckskin, but the man had not stopped at the livery. Raider thanked him and saddled up.

What next?

He'd have to get back to the ranch. He wondered if he should wait until Sanders was ready to ride. He could act as a bodyguard at least; although he didn't see any sign of a threat. Unless—

He wondered about Mrs. Sanders again. Why wasn't she at

her husband's side in the last days of the campaign? Maybe John
Sanders didn't want her there. Maybe he had found out about her
cheating ways.

"Damn it all."

"What's that?" the livery man asked.

Raider shook his head. "Nothin'."

Damn it all, there was something going on. Raider felt the
itching, like a wound that hadn't healed all the way. All the parts
were there, they just weren't put together in the right order.
Maybe he'd get some answers at the Green Sands Ranch. It
seemed like the only place left to look.

The ranch house was quiet as Raider approached on the stallion. Two lights burned inside the place. One upstairs and one in
the kitchen. Raider tied his mount at the hitching post in back. He
wasn't sure what he would find inside; probably nothing, he
thought. Unless the lady of the house was up and around.

"That you, cowboy?"

The back door opened. Tillie, the cook, stuck her head out.
She had a meat cleaver in hand.

Raider assured her that she was in no danger. Said he just rode
in from town. He was going to wait for Mr. Sanders to get home.

Tillie shook her head. "Cain't tell what's gonna happen dese
days. I been feelin' hateful in my bones. Don't like it much."

Raider stepped up into the kitchen, following the black
woman.

"You want some food, cowboy?"

"Sure 'nuff, Tillie. I ain't 'et in a while. What you got on the
stove t'day?"

"Stew. And some cornbread. You'se lucky I ain't cleaned the
kitchen yet. Had me a long day."

Raider took off his hat and sat down at the kitchen table. "I
know just what you mean, Tillie."

"Where you been anyways?"

He shrugged. "I been walkin' in mud an' I ain't even got dirty
boots t' show for it."

She put the plate of stew and cornbread in front of him. "What
de devil you talkin' 'bout?"

"Nothin'."

He started to eat.

Tillie stood there, watching. "Can I sit wid you?"

"Why not?"

"Some white fokes don' cotton to sittin' at de same table wid us colored people. You know dat's so."

He gestured to the other chair. "Take a load off."

She smiled, bending toward him a little. "You wan' some whiskey?"

"Sure."

"I likes me a liddle nip in de evenin'. I'll fetch two cups."

Raider had finished his meal by the time she came back with the whiskey. They never got to drink it. Mrs. Sanders burst into the kitchen, clad in a flowing white robe.

"Well," she said, smiling at Raider. "I thought I heard somebody ride up. I was hoping it might be my husband."

Raider looked away. "I bet you were."

She turned indignantly toward the kitchen door. "Well, if you're going to be rude, then I'll just say good night."

"Say it twice if it makes you feel better."

Mrs. Sanders stormed out of the kitchen, heading back to her bedroom.

Tillie laughed. "Ain' never seen nobody git under dat woman's skin de way you do, cowboy."

Raider leaned back in the chair. "She been goin' out at night, Tillie?"

"I ain' one to be gossipin', cowboy. You wan' some of dat whiskey?"

He waved her off. "Not t'night. Think I'll go on up an' get some rest. If you see Mr. Sanders when he comes in, tell him t' wake me up."

"I'll do dat."

Raider was halfway up the stairs when he heard the man's voice.

"Good evening, sir. Will you be needing any assistance?"

He turned back to look at Dennison, who stood at the bottom of the stairs. "Yeah, I could use some help. Come on up."

When they were standing in the bedroom, Raider pointed a finger at the butler. "Now look here, Dennison, I 'bout had it with your tight lip. If you got any notions as t' what's goin' on 'round here, I want you t' go ahead an' tell me right now."

"Sir, I—"

"No more bullshit, Dennison. Either you talk or I whip your skinny ass right here an' now."

The butler took a deep breath. "Very well, sir. If you insist on threatening me with violence, I suppose I have no choice."

Raider felt sort of bad about bullying the man, but he figured Dennison might shed some light on John Sanders.

"What is it you wish to know, sir?"

"Do you know why Sanders hired me?"

The butler nodded. "Yes. To find that outlaw who's using his former moniker. Have you had any luck?"

"I'm askin' the questions, Dennison. Does Sanders really think this man Sonora is gonna do him dirty?"

"I suppose, sir. I haven't quite been able to make the connection myself. It would seem so on the outside, but so far nothing has come of it. I suppose it could be coincidence. There hasn't been any trouble here."

Raider shook his head. "Damn it all, there don't seem t' be much cause for me t' be here. But somethin's wrong. I can feel it."

"Did you see Mr. Sanders in town, sir?"

"Yeah, he's in there buyin' drinks for ever'body. Jenkins was doin' the same thing earlier t'day. Both of 'em are sluggin' it out afore the election next week."

"Hmm."

Raider looked at him. "What about Mrs. Sanders?"

"I beg your pardon, sir?"

"Don't play pussyfoot with me, Dennison. Has the woman o' the house been sneakin' out at night?"

"No more than usual," the butler replied dryly.

"What's that s'posed t' mean?"

Dennison sniffed a little. "Come, come, sir. You must've witnessed it for yourself."

"Don't much get by you, does it?"

"I pick and choose what I see, sir."

Raider exhaled dejectedly. "Is she seein' Jenkins?"

"Who, sir?"

"Jenkins!" the big man cried. "You know, the boy that her husband is runnin' 'gainst in the election."

"Why, I don't know." He seemed genuinely puzzled. "I mean, I've never seen them together. I just know that she has the occasional rendezvous behind the barn. I've never witnessed it personally."

"Has she been out t' see him lately?"

Dennison thought about it for a moment. "No, sir. Not since you left the last time. She's stayed in her room since then."

"Layin' low," Raider replied. "She figgers I'll tell her husband. She's waitin' till after the election."

"I suppose so, sir."

Raider squinted at the manservant. "You don't seem too upset about all this, Dennison."

"A good butler never allows his emotions to come into play, sir. I'd like to say good night if that's to your liking."

"Yeah. Go on."

Dennison left quickly.

Raider lay back on the bed, looking at the ceiling. What to do next? He figured it would be better to dismiss himself from the case as soon as Sanders got home. Hell, there really wasn't a case when you looked at it. Johnny Sonora was using Sanders's old name, but that didn't seem to mean much.

Something bumped the wall outside his room.

Raider sat up, reaching for his Colt. Somebody stepped past his door, heading for the stairs. He got up to have a look. When he peeked out, he saw Mrs. Sanders exiting through the front door.

He hurried after her, following her all the way to the barn.

Mrs. Sanders stopped behind the barn, waiting for her lover, no doubt.

Raider climbed into the hayloft and waited with her.

It wasn't long before he heard the approaching horse. The man climbed out of the saddle, embracing Ellen Sanders. Raider squinted, trying to see the man's face. It was too dark to see him clearly.

"Kiss me, Franklin."

They kissed for a while, until things got hotter. Then they were rolling around on the ground. Raider decided not to surprise them. It really wasn't any of his business. Sanders hadn't hired him to catch a cheating wife, even if she was diddling his political adversary.

He climbed down from the loft and went back to the house.

An hour later, Mrs. Sanders returned, ascending the stairs to her bedchamber. Raider had to wonder why a young man like Franklin Jenkins would jeopardize his whole life for a woman like Ellen Sanders. It just didn't seem to make sense. Hell, nothing in this case made sense.

Maybe John Sanders could help him piece it all together. Nothing to do but wait. He fell back on the bed again, closing his eyes, sleeping until he heard the knock at the door the next morning.

CHAPTER FIFTEEN

Dennison called from the hallway. "Sir, Mr. Sanders is waiting for you in his office."

Raider rolled over and looked at the door. "He is, huh? He better have a jug o' coffee waitin' for me."

"I'll see to it," the butler replied.

Raider eased his feet to the floor, sitting on the edge of the bed. It was foggy for a few minutes, but then it all came back to him. He had to see the man who had hired him, to set Sanders straight on a couple of things. He wondered how Sanders would take the news about his wife and his political opponent. Sometimes clients didn't like hearing bad tidings. And they always seemed to blame Raider for telling them the truth.

He got dressed and started for Sanders's office.

The old gent was waiting impatiently for him. He told Raider to enter when he knocked on the door. Raider sat down in a wooden chair on the other side of Sanders's desk.

Dennison entered with coffee before they said anything. Raider welcomed a steaming cup of the hot, black liquid. Sanders declined the coffee, dismissing his butler with a snap of the fingers. Raider flinched at the demeaning gesture that didn't seem to faze Dennison. He liked Dennison and didn't enjoy seeing him get treated like dirt.

"Now," Sanders said, "I suppose you came back to Stockton because you have something to tell me."

The big man scowled at the rancher. "I came back t' Stockton 'cause I followed the California Kid here."

Sanders's face went white. "Do you have any idea why he's come here?"

"Seems t' think he's gonna strike it big in these parts. I never heard him say exac'ly why he b'lieves the rainbow ends here. An' he's definitely usin' your name, Sanders. But he denies ever hearin' o' you."

"Well, he could be lying!" exclaimed the wide-eyed rancher. "I knew it. He's come here to hurt me."

"Mebbe. Mebbe not."

Sanders glared at him. "What else have you learned about this outlaw?"

Raider grimaced, leaning back a little. "I hate t' disappoint you, Sanders, but I ain't found nothin' t' show me that Johnny Sonora is a outlaw."

"Hasn't he killed other men?"

"Yeah, but he always lets 'em draw first. Sometimes the kid provokes it, sometimes he don't. Sometimes punks just come lookin' for anybody with a reputation. Sonora sure as hell don't have no trouble cuttin' 'em down."

"I could still have him arrested," Sanders offered. "The sheriff would take him in and he could be tried."

Raider gulped the rest of the coffee and scowled at Sanders. "Well, you got two problems with that, sir."

"Two?"

"Catchin' him an' tryin' him," Raider replied. "First, you gotta catch him. And that's gonna mean a posse. Now, you can probably bring him in, but if the kid d'cides t' fight, he's gonna kill a bunch o' people afore you kill him. An' hell, even if you did put the net on him, there ain't enough evidence t' convict him in a fair trial."

Sanders slammed his fist into his palm. "Damn. He's free to roam. To ruin me in this election."

Raider took a deep breath, thinking that it was best just to go on and say it. Sanders was going to scream like a stuck hog, but he had to listen. Raider hoped he had read things right. He had to say how it looked to him.

"Mr. Sanders, you ain't gonna like this, but I have reason to b'lieve that your wife is messin' 'round with the man who's runnin' 'gainst you in the mayor race."

Sanders frowned for a second, but then his face slacked into a condescending smile. "You're crazy, Raider."

"Twice I heard her meet him out b'hind the barn," the big man went on. "She calls him Franklin. Met him last night."

"That's insane," Sanders cried. "Franklin Jenkins was in town last night. I saw him with my own two eyes."

"Did you see him 'bout midnight?"

"Well, I—"

"You didn't," Raider accused. "'Cause he was in back o' the barn rollin' on the ground with your wife."

For a moment, Raider thought the red-faced rancher was going to challenge him to a fist fight. Sanders bristled like a wild razorback protecting its young. But then he put his face in his hands and started to cry.

Raider waited a long time before the teary gentleman looked up again. "I know this hurts, Sanders, but—"

The rancher waved him off. "Don't you think I know about Ellen? I try to keep it quiet. All right, she's seeing someone. But what does that have to do with Johnny Sonora and the fact that he's the California Kid?"

The big man straightened in the chair. "Say this, Sanders. Say Jenkins wants to discredit you. Say he's in love with your wife. He wants t' d'stroy you, put you as low as you can go. He pays this kid t' become your old self. Sonora had money, plenty of it, and I'm bettin' he ain't done honest labor for a coon's age."

"I thought you said he wasn't an outlaw."

"He ain't yet," Raider replied. "But he's on his way. No, he came t' Stockton for a reason. Made it slow from the north. Took his time, but he did manage to get here in time for the election."

Sanders nodded. "Yes, I see what you mean."

"When Sonora saw Jenkins in town, he made a big stink, sayin' how he hates stump-thumpers. It could've been a act t' deny he's in with Jenkins."

The rancher frowned. "Stump-thumpers?"

"Politicians."

Sanders smiled slightly. "Yes—but no! I can't believe that

Franklin Jenkins is in on this. It doesn't make sense. He's one of the most decent, honest, Christian men that I've ever known."

"Sounds like you're friends with him."

"We've never been close friends," the rancher replied, "but I've always respected him. He's been fair in this election."

"So far," the big man chimed in.

Sanders sighed. "So what do we do? Wait around for this kid to make his move?"

"Sonora ain't the one I wanna flush outta the bushes," Raider said. "At least not yet."

"Then who? Surely you don't expect to go after Jenkins."

Raider nodded. "That's him. Only I want t' do it in my own way. An' I want you t' help me."

Sanders's eyes narrowed. "Don't be ridiculous. You can't go into town and just challenge Jenkins."

"Jenkins is gonna come t' us, Mr. Sanders. See, we got the bait. She's right up there in her bedroom, preenin' like a rich man's cat."

The rancher waved his hand. "I won't allow it. I don't care what Ellen has done, I still can't get her involved in something that would hurt her."

"You ain't got any choice, Sanders. Not if you really wanna know the truth 'bout all this shit."

Sanders leaned forward on his desk. "You're probably wondering how I can be so tolerant of Ellen."

"Ain't none o' my business—"

"I wasn't a saint in my younger days," Sanders went on. "I had women. Lots of them. And believe it or not, I loved one or two of them. There was even one who—but the war came. And here I am, paying for what I did."

Raider said he wasn't interested in who had to pay for what. He just wanted to put it all together. It might fit. Then again, he might be totally wrong about everything.

Sanders gawked at him. "So you're willing to admit that you might be wrong about Franklin Jenkins being at the bottom of all this?"

Raider shrugged. "I been wrong afore. But there's only one way t' catch a rabbit. You gotta lay the snare."

"And you think Ellen is the bait."

"Yes, sir, I do. But I can't do it without you."

Sanders gave a slight nod. "All right. What do you want me to do?"

Raider rubbed his hands together. "Thanks, boss. Now listen up. First, you gotta tell your wife that you're goin' outta town on business. Tell her you're runnin' down t' Manteca for a day. Take Dennison an' Tillie with you. I'll stay on t' protect Mrs. Sanders, but I'll see to it that I ain't around very much."

"What good will that do? She won't meet her lover if she knows you're on the premises."

Raider shook his head. "Naw, she ain't afraid o' me. She thinks I won't tell you 'bout her meetin' with this boy."

"And you really think she'll go to meet him?"

"It's our best shot right now. If there's a connection b'tween Jenkins an' Sonora an' your wife, we can ask the man firsthand after we catch him in the act so t' speak. He'll be so s'prised that he'll prob'ly talk."

Sanders lifted a finger to the sky. "Yes! And when the citizens of Stockton find out that he's been seeing my wife behind my back, I'm sure they won't vote for him."

"I wondered how long it was gonna take for you to figger that out."

Sanders threw up his hands. "But what the hell are you going to do about the California Kid?"

"You can stick close t' the ranch," the big man offered. "An' I'll go with you when you go into town."

"What if he confronts me on the way to Manteca?"

Raider stood up. "You ain't goin' t' Manteca. You're gonna send Tillie an' Dennison into Stockton an' then you're gonna double back t' meet me. I want you there when I disturb the two lovebirds."

"I'm still leery of this kid, Raider. He sure as hell hasn't shown up here by accident."

Raider had to agree with that statement, even if it was a little obvious. He told Sanders that they would have to be patient. Just sit it out and see what happened. Things would look a whole lot different when they finally caught Franklin Jenkins red-handed.

"This is absurd!" cried John Sanders. "It's almost midnight and we haven't heard anything but a barn owl!"

Raider sat on the pile of straw in the hayloft, watching the ground below. It was the spot where Mrs. Sanders had met her illicit beau the last two times. Raider wondered if they were going to rendezvous for another night of adulterous love.

"This is a waste of time," Sanders went on. "Nobody's coming. I tell you, I'm going back into the house."

Raider stopped him. "Sanders, we gotta see it through. If you wanna fire me an' take me off the case, that's diff'rent. But you can't forget that Sonora is somewhere in the area. And he might be out t' get you."

The air seemed to leave Sanders. It was always different when your own life was on the line. That made the most careless man cautious or the most cowardly brave. It made things clear, sometimes.

Raider looked down again. "I hope it wasn't too much."

"What are you talking about?"

"The whole show," Raider offered. "How did she look when you said you were leavin'?"

"She took it well," Sanders replied sarcastically. "She didn't seem surprised. Just bored."

"Ya gotta keep 'em happy," Raider said. "It comes with the terr'tory."

Sanders let out a deep breath. "You know, she's been a fairly good wife to me. I—"

"Go to the front o' the loft," Raider said quickly, to cut him off. "See if the light in her room is still burnin'."

Sanders reluctantly obeyed the big man's order.

"Yes, it's still burning," he called from the other side of the barn.

"Stay there an' watch!"

Sanders sat down, peering toward his own house. At least he would be out of Raider's hair for a while. Best to enjoy the silence.

"This is a waste of time!" Sanders called again.

"Shh. She'll hear you."

They were quiet for a while.

Raider listened, hoping for the sounds of hooves on dirt. He wondered how Ellen Sanders got word to her lover. Could she summon him on such short notice? What if they had to wait another day for him to come? Raider could have a note sent from her husband, saying that Sanders wasn't coming back for the rest of the week. They might have to sit for a few days until the woodchuck stuck its head out of the hole.

He heard movement in the straw. Sanders was tiptoeing across the loft. Had he decided to give up?

"I thought I told you t' watch the house," Raider said.

"She's coming!" Sanders replied. "She left the house and she's heading this way."

Raider lifted his Colt from his pocket. He checked to make sure that five chambers were filled with lead. No need for the sixth, not on something like this.

The rancher gaped at the weapon. "What's that for?"

"In case things get outta hand," Raider replied. "Don't worry. Nobody's gonna get hurt on this."

"Is that a guarantee, Raider?"

"As close as I can get, Sanders. As close as I can get."

Ellen Sanders situated herself just below them. She was wearing a fine white gown and her perfume rose on the night air. Raider watched her, making Sanders stay back. He didn't want the husband to have to witness it firsthand. And when her lover came, Raider planned to break it up before things got really steamy. He owed that to Sanders.

The low echo of hooves came off the plain.

Mrs. Sanders stiffened, peering into the darkness.

The man rode up on a palomino mare. He climbed out of the saddle and put his arms around her. They kissed for a long time.

"Franklin," she said when they broke off, "I've missed you so much. I'll be in pain every day until the election."

"Can't we tell him now, Ellen?" the man replied.

Raider grimaced. That wasn't a familiar voice. It didn't sound like the man he heard in town on speech day.

He motioned to Sanders and then pointed to his ear.

The rancher slid closer to the wall, looking down through a crack.

"Is that Jenkins?" Raider asked.

Sanders frowned and then shrugged.

Raider listened, but they were kissing again. He wondered if they might go to the house since nobody was home. A warm bed sure beat the hell out of humping on the damp ground.

"I can't stay long," the man said. "I have to get back to Stockton. Are you going to keep your promise to me after the election?"

"Yes," Ellen Sanders replied. "I won't let you down."

Raider looked at Sanders. "You heard enough?"

The man nodded.

Raider stood up.

"What are you going to do?"

Raider lifted the pistol in front of him. "This."

He kicked open the loft door and grabbed the bale line that dangled next to the wall. A rebel yell escaped from his lungs, startling the two people below him. Raider leaped out of the loft into the darkness. He sailed down from the sky, landing on Mrs. Sanders's boyfriend, knocking him unconscious at the end of his flight.

Raider rolled the unconscious man over. "There he is."

John Sanders lifted an oil lamp. "That's not Franklin Jenkins!"

Raider frowned. "No. No, it's not."

They both looked at Ellen Sanders who was cowering against the wall.

Sanders demanded to know the identity of the man on the ground.

Mrs. Sanders began to cry.

Raider shook his head. "This may take a while. Let's get 'em both back up t' the house."

"She's hysterical," Sanders said.

"Get a couple o' whiskeys in her an' she'll be all right. Come on, help me get this man over the saddle o' his mount. I don't wanna carry him all the way back t' the house."

"What about Ellen?"

"You can walk with her yourself, Sanders. I mean, she is your wife after all."

When Raider got the unconscious man back to the house, he laid him out on one of the sofas in the parlor. He searched the man's pockets but didn't find anything to give him a clue as to the man's identity. Why the hell had Mrs. Sanders been calling him Franklin?

Sanders led his wife into the parlor a few minutes later.

Raider sat her down and made her take a couple of swallows of brandy. He and Sanders had a shot as well. The liquor took the edge off. Ellen Sanders looked at the man on the sofa.

"Is he dead?" she asked.

Raider shook his head. "No. But he's gonna have a headache for a while. Who is he, Ellen?"

"Nobody. Just a man I met in Stockton."

Sanders gaped at her. "Why were you calling him Franklin?"

"I don't have to tell you," she replied.

"If you want to continue being my wife, you'll tell me this instant!" Sanders demanded.

Her eyes widened. "You mean, you won't leave me after this?"

"I want all the facts," Sanders said.

Raider nodded. "That's a good start, Mrs. Sanders. Why don't you tell me why you're sneakin' 'round with this man?"

She sighed, laughing a little. "I'm not sneaking around with him," she replied. "He's just a dupe. Somebody I paid to impersonate Franklin Jenkins."

Sanders frowned at her. "Why would you do something like that?"

"I wanted the Pinkerton here to get the idea that I was seeing Franklin Jenkins on the sly. That's the only time I met that man. When Raider was here to see me."

"How'd you signal him?" Raider asked.

She shrugged. "I paid him to come every night for two weeks. He'd sit out there and wait for me. I'd swing a lamp in the window."

Raider nodded appreciatively. "Makes sense. But why did you want me t' think you an' Franklin Jenkins was—"

"Because I thought it might help John win the election. You see, when I realized that you wouldn't tell John about me being a flirt, I assumed that you wouldn't tell him about me seeing Franklin Jenkins—not directly anyway—and I thought John would never listen if you did say things about me."

"I don't want to hear anymore!" Sanders shouted.

Raider looked at the wife. "I do. Keep goin', honey."

She frowned at him. "I never thought you'd interfere with me and my would-be lover. But I did think you'd spread gossip all over town. When everybody heard that I was carrying on with Jenkins, the whole town would have to have sympathy for John. They'd have to elect him mayor. That's the last chance he had. But I played it all wrong."

"You surely did," her husband rejoined. "Now go upstairs and stay in your room."

"Not so fast," Raider said. "I have a few more questions that I'd like t' ask the little lady."

Sanders started to protest.

Ellen waved him off. "No, John. I'll answer anything that this big clod has to ask. Go on, Pinkerton. Do your worst."

Raider gestured to John Sanders. "Did you know your hubby here used t' be called the California Kid?"

She looked at her husband. "Really?"

"He was a big time gunfighter," Raider went on. "Only now somebody else has started usin' his old name. You wouldn't know anythin' 'bout that, would you, Mrs. Sanders?"

"No. John? You were really a gunfighter?"

Raider watched her closely. She seemed genuinely surprised. But then, she had almost pulled off the bogus scam with her hired lover. She was still not a woman to be taken lightly.

"That night we rode down from Frisco," Raider went on, "there was three men at the station depot waitin' for us. They was out t' get me. Somebody hired 'em not long after I was hired by your husband. Do you know anythin' 'bout that, lady?"

She shook her head. "No. Why would I want to kill you? I just wanted you to spread a little rumor and you wouldn't even do that!"

"I always have been the tight-lipped kind."

They were silent for a few moments.

Raider hit another shot of the brandy.

Sanders was looking at his wife. Raider could see that the old boy really did care about her. She was just too much for him to handle. Too much for any man that wasn't ready to have his heart broken.

He had one more question for her. "What d' you know about Johnny Sonora? The California Kid?"

"I never heard of him until now," she replied. "Who is he?"

"He's fast with a gun," Sanders said. "I hired Raider to find him and learn why he was using my old name. I'm not proud of my gunfighting days, Ellen. I've always tried to feel that my service in the war more than made up for those hateful times. I'm sorry."

She smiled at him. "I'm the one who should be apologizing, John. I just wanted to help you. I know it was stupid, but I—"

"No, Ellen, let's just stop right here. No more regrets. If you want to stay on here with me, I'll see to it that you have all the things that you're accustomed to. I won't hold any of this against you."

"Do you really mean that, John?"

He nodded. "I love you, Ellen. If you want to stay, I'm opening my arms to you."

Raider thought it was a little too mushy. She ran to her husband and threw her arms around him, planting kisses on his face. Sanders lapped it up like a dog. Raider still wasn't sure if he believed her improbable story. She was too cagey to be dismissed.

"I'll be waiting upstairs for you," she said to her husband. "Don't be too late coming to bed."

She flowed out of the room with a newfound dignity and spirit.

Sanders looked sheepishly at Raider. "I know you probably don't have much respect for me right now, but I—"

"None o' my business," Raider replied.

"You think she's telling the truth about this man?"

"Mebbe."

Sanders shook his head. "That would be like Ellen to try something so unlikely. She's right about one thing. I don't have a prayer of winning this election."

"That ain't important, Sanders."

"No?"

Raider stood up, turning to the window. "Johnny Sonora is still out there an' he's still usin' your old name. Now I'm guessin' that somebody put him up to it. They're payin' him t' play the game. An' the way it looks, nobody can be ruled out. Somebody hired the California Kid an' I still have t' find out who an' why."

"I have something to say about that," Sanders intoned. "After all, I'm the one who brought you into this. I can fire you any time I want to."

Raider shrugged. "Suits me. But you're the one who might have his life on the line. If I leave, you better get some protection."

Sanders put a hand on his chest. "Do you really think that I'm in danger?"

"I can't say yes or no, honcho. But I still ain't got t' the bottom o' all this an' I ain't gonna be satisfied till I do. Now what's it gonna be? Are you keepin' me on the case?"

Sanders thought about it and finally nodded. "All right. You can stay. But I don't want you interfering in my campaign or my personal life. Is that clear?"

"Clear as Montana rain, Mr. Sanders."

The big man turned toward the unconscious lump on the sofa.

"What are you doing, Raider?"

"I wanna see that this one wakes up on the range. I'm gonna tell him not t' come 'round here no more. I'll scare him enough t' make sure he don't do this agin, at least not here."

Sanders agreed that was a good idea.

He helped Raider with the body, dropping it sideways over the saddle again. "What are you going to do after you get rid of this one?" Sanders asked.

"I'm gonna look for the man who's payin' Johnny Sonora."

"And then?"

Raider chortled. "Well, I'll either shoot him or ask him why he wanted t' hire the California Kid."

That was the best way to take care of it. Plain and simple. Now all he had to do was find the right place to start hunting.

CHAPTER SIXTEEN

Raider tilted his canteen, pouring water on the face of the unconscious man. The cool liquid splashed over the man, waking him from his sleep. He made a funny noise with his mouth. Then he coughed and cried out.

"Take it easy," Raider said.

The man squirmed on the saddle. Raider had tied his hands with a rope under the horse's belly. He couldn't dismount until the big man cut him free.

"Where the hell am I?" the man asked.

"You're headin' south," Raider replied. "After I ask you a few questions."

"And what if I don't want to answer your questions?"

"Then you're goin' south, only you'll be goin' belly-down on that saddle. It won't be but a couple o' days afore somebody finds you. You might even run into somebody by tomorrow mornin'."

The man groaned. "You wouldn't do that."

"Try me, pardner."

A long silence and then a sigh. "All right. What do you want to know?"

"Tell me 'bout you an' the woman."

137

"Oh yeah. I almost forgot. She hired me. Said I was supposed to sit out on the range there and watch her window. If she swung the lantern, I went in to play her lover."

"How much was she payin' you?"

"Hundred a week," the man replied. "I tell ya, it wasn't that bad either. She could kiss. I had worse jobs."

Raider still thought it sounded harebrained. "She give you any clues as to why she hired you?"

"Said her husband was hirin' some hotshot Pinkerton to spy on her. Said she planned to give everyone somethin' to talk about."

"She never mentioned hiring a kid named Johnny Sonora, did she?"

The man shook his head, groaning. "Nooo. Look here, cut me down, pardner. I ain't even packin' a gun. I'll ride on. Hell, I was tired of that job anyway."

Raider laughed a little. "You tellin' me you got tired of kissin' Mrs. Sanders?"

"She wouldn't let me have anything else. We just rolled around a little. Buddy, I can tell you that I wanted some of that too. She's fine. Got great big—"

"Yeah, I get the drift."

The man laughed back at him. "Sounds like you thought about it too."

"Look here, honcho. She ever say anythin' 'bout the man you were s'posed to be impersonatin'?"

"You mean Franklin? I heard of the man who's runnin' for mayor. I reckon it had somethin' to do with that. I never really asked. I needed that hundred a week. I lost everything I had when I was prospectin'."

"You ever hear of the California Kid?"

"No, I swear. Never."

Raider moved his mount a little closer to the hog-tied gentleman. "I'm gonna cut you loose, honcho."

"Glory be!"

"But you're gonna ride south an' you're gonna keep away from Stockton. You got that?"

The man nodded eagerly. "I surely will."

"Besides," Raider added, "Mr. Sanders is gonna be lookin' for you after you was foolin' with his wife. You might do better t' head back east a little ways. Get out o' California."

"Mister, you cut me loose and I'll get the hell out of this godforsaken territory as fast as this nag will carry me."

Raider dipped with the knife, severing the man's bonds in one swipe of the blade.

The man tumbled onto the ground, landing with a thud.

Raider watched him, keeping his hand on his Colt to make sure the man wasn't going for some hidden weapon. "You okay, honcho?"

The man nodded, rising to his feet. He swung into the saddle and turned his mount west. Raider drew his Colt and fired two shots to get the mount moving in the right direction. The man charged off into the dark, hopefully to never be seen again by the tall Pinkerton.

Raider reined his mount, turning back toward Green Sands Ranch. He let the stallion walk slowly. The animal deserved a rest. It was only a few miles back to the ranch house, but Raider also wanted to think about things.

His first priority was making sure that Sanders and the ranch were safe. He'd have to call in the ranch hands, maybe hire a few more men. Ride some patrols, keep guards at the front and back of the house. Men in the barn with rifles. Men on the roof with scatterguns. He wondered if Sanders was ready to meet the expense of more protection.

Damn it, he thought, the California Kid was going to make some sort of move. He had to be linked to the current matters at hand. Why else would he be using Sanders's old name? And why would he be staying in Stockton if he wasn't up to something? It would probably come before the election.

He'd have to sleep on it. Get back to the ranch and make sure things were secure. Everything else could wait until morning.

Sanders went for Raider's scheme to beef up his crew for more protection. By midafternoon, the rancher had assembled fifteen of his own hands as well as another seven hired on just for their guns. He gave them a short speech and turned them over to Raider.

The big man from Arkansas quickly gave them their assignments. Four men at the house, three at the barn and the rest to ride patrols in all directions. It really couldn't have worked out better.

"I just wanna say one thing," he told them finally, "you all got a description o' the kid. Blond hair and sorta skinny. Now if you find him, don't try t' take him. He's fast. An' there's no need for you t' kill him. Not yet, anyways."

"He can't be that fast," someone said.

Raider drew his Colt. "He's faster'n me."

That made them cautious. Nobody wanted to draw on the big man and they surely didn't want to face anybody faster. It surprised Raider to hear himself say it. But he knew it was true. One on one, Johnny Sonora probably had a quicker gun hand.

"Now go on and do what you're bein' paid t' do."

They didn't have to be told twice.

Sanders stepped up next to Raider. "If you think we'll need more men, I'll be happy to hire them."

"This'll be all right. I got ever'body workin' t'gether. They'll all take turns, switch jobs around so it won't be too dull."

"I'd settle for dull," Sanders replied.

The rancher was sweating. Raider felt the heat himself. He planned to ride his own patrols, day and night. His men had mirrors to signal each other when the sun was up. They'd use torches in the dark.

"Anybody ridin' in here is gonna get spotted," Raider told Sanders. "An' then we close in. Like a Missouri River fish trap. Catch him first an' then talk t' him."

"I hope so."

"How many days afore the election?"

Sanders exhaled. "Five. You think he's going to move before then?"

"If that's what he's been hired t' do."

"I'm going inside to get some rest," the rancher replied. "And I don't want Ellen to be alarmed by all this."

"She oughta feel safe," Raider replied sarcastically. "I know I do."

Sanders pointed a finger at him. "I can still fire you. I have enough men to protect me until the election."

Raider shrugged. "You can hand me my walkin' papers any time."

"No. Just keep your yap shut."

He stormed inside, leaving Raider on the porch.

The big man couldn't blame him for being so angry. Sanders had endured a lot in the past few days. Lady Luck had flipped the old boy's life back and forth like a day-old flapjack. And on top of it all, Sanders was probably going to lose the election too.

Raider started for the barn. He had decided that three men were not needed there. Two could watch the back of the spread just as well. One of the others could grab a horse and ride with Raider.

He hadn't gotten very far from the house when the man on the roof called to him. He turned back to see what had happened. The sentry shouted that one of the search parties was signaling with a mirror from the south.

"That didn't take long," the big man said to himself.

He found his mount and rode hard toward the flashing light.

When Raider rode up on the three men, he saw that they were all bent over looking at the trail. He dismounted and stared at the fresh tracks. They were heading due north, but then they abruptly turned west, toward a low-lying cluster of hills.

"We saw him, Mr. Raider. He was comin' straight for us. Then he turned toward the hills."

Raider gazed to the west. "Is there one clear trail through there?"

"Yeah, it comes out north of here, just the other side of the ridge."

"What kind of horse was he ridin'?"

"A buckskin."

Raider whistled. "Did you see the rider?"

"Not up close."

A buckskin heading due north, for Sanders's place. The kid had arrived. Now all they had to do was catch him.

Raider pointed toward the hills. "You two, follow his tracks. See if you can catch up with him. Don't take him, just make sure he goes toward the end of the trail."

"What're you gonna do?"

"Me and this man here will head north, take the long way 'round, see if we can cut him off. That sound possible t' you?"

The man nodded appreciatively. "You should be able to make it there before he does. The ground is flatter and you don't have to worry about the hills. Gonna get dark though, in a couple of hours."

Raider swung into the saddle. "Then we better get goin'."

The rest of them mounted up and they started after the buckskin.

Raider and the other rider reached the north end of the hill trail just before dusk. They positioned themselves on opposite sides of the path, waiting. Raider hoped the buckskin would come up the road before all the light vanished from the hills. It would be hard to catch the kid in the dark. But night fell before anyone emerged on the path. Raider waited and listened. He watched the dark shadows between the trees, wondering if the kid would travel after sundown. He got his answer when the tiny fire began to glow. He picked up his Winchester and started down.

Raider was moving toward the path when he heard the hoot owl call. It was the signal from the other man, who had also seen the fire. Had the two men who were following the kid seen it too?

He joined his compatriot on the trail. "How far down you think he is?"

"Not even a quarter mile."

"All right," the big man said, "you double back. Don't let him hear you. See if you can find your two buddies. Y'all cover me from the south. I'm gonna go in on him."

"You sure you want to go alone?"

Raider nodded. "No need for all of us t' get killed. If you hear shootin', you get the other two an' blast that son of a bitch with your rifles. You hear me?"

The man nodded and started off down the trail. Raider was right behind him. He stalked the campfire, wondering which way to go in. He crept around until he could see the figure sitting in the circle of the fire's light. The kid's back was to him.

He heard the buckskin snorting. The animal pawed the earth a little. The man by the fire looked to both sides.

Raider crouched low. Why did the damned horse have to act up? It was going to be harder to take the kid now.

He started toward the camp.

Suddenly the kid leaped up and kicked out the fire. The coals went everywhere. Raider started to aim his Winchester, but there was nothing to shoot at. He didn't even hear the kid moving.

Then the buckskin was running past him, heading toward the trail. He let off a shot but the animal just kept running. Damn. He would never catch him on foot.

He was turning back toward his own mount when he heard the shots. Rifles kicked up in the night. They were so close that he could see three muzzle flashes. Then somebody called his name.

"We got him!" echoed through the hills.

The kid had run straight into the three men who had been riding with Raider. He wondered if they had killed Sonora. He rushed along the path until he reached them.

"Is he dead?" the big man asked.

"No, but he sure as hell fell off that buckskin."

Raider looked down at the man. "Son of a bitch. One of you boys got a match?"

The sulphur match glowed to life. Raider grabbed it and held it over the fallen man. He cursed out loud. Another surprise.

"What's wrong, Raider?"

"That ain't Johnny Sonora," the big man replied.

He shook out the flame and told the others to build a fire.

The man on the ground groaned a little as he stirred back to consciousness. Raider lifted him to his feet. The man staggered on wobbly legs, leaning on the tall Pinkerton.

"You okay, pardner?"

The man gaped at him. "What the hell is goin' on? What happened?"

"Just a little mix-up," Raider said. "You heard me comin' so you lit out. I thought you was somebody else."

A fire lit up the countryside again. The fallen man sat down and told them his name was Hinton. He had ridden north from Manteca. Had heard that somebody at the Green Sands was looking for hands. But when he saw four riders coming at him, he had run, thinking they were outlaws.

Raider thought that all sounded logical. He asked if anybody had whiskey. One of the other riders had a bottle in his saddlebag. They all shared it and good feelings were restored.

"We're awful sorry," Raider said. "We thought you was somebody else. Where'd you buy that buckskin, anyway?"

Hinton chortled. "Manteca. Bought it off this kid. He was pretty tough. Killed a man while I was there."

Raider straightened his body. "Kid? Was he blond?"

Hinton nodded. "Yeah. Sold me the buckskin cheap when I told him I was ridin' up this way."

"Sonora," Raider said. "When he killed that man—did the kid draw first?"

"No, the other one drew first. But the kid was too fast."

"You didn't even see his hand move, did you?" Raider offered.

Hinton stared into the fire. "No, I didn't even see his hand move."

Raider got up and grabbed one of the mounts. "I'm headin' back t' the ranch. You boys take care o' Hinton."

"What's your hurry?"

"Because this could all be a trap," Raider replied. "Sonora could've sold this man his horse because he knew we'd chase him."

"But—"

Raider didn't have time to talk. He urged the horse along the narrow trail, heading for Green Sands. He was afraid of what he might find when he got there.

But there was nothing wrong at the ranch. Raider rode in to see the sentries stationed in their places. The others riding patrols had come in for the night. No sign of Johnny Sonora.

He went straight to Sanders's office, banging on the door.

"Come in!"

Raider pushed into the brightly lighted chamber. "Sonora is in Manteca."

Sanders frowned. "How do you know?"

"We found a boy campin' on the northern edge o' your property. He said he bought Sonora's horse a couple o' days ago. Said Sonora had already killed one man in Manteca."

"Are you going after him?" Sanders asked.

Raider shrugged. "I could. But it wouldn't make much sense. I wouldn't feel right if I killed him for no reason. I mean, he hasn't really done nothin' t' you, Mr. Sanders."

"You aren't scared of him, are you?"

Raider nodded. "A little. The way you're scared of a rattler when you hear him afore you see him."

"I don't like it," Sanders said. "Four more days until the election. Why hasn't he come after me?"

"Mebbe he don't want you."

The rancher scowled at him. "Then what the hell does he want?"

"We gotta stay put, Sanders. He'll come to us if he wants trouble. We got four days t' wait. If it's gonna happen, then it'll probably happen b'tween now an' then."

"You stay close to me, Raider."

"If that's what you want, Mr. Sanders. You got a handgun?"

Sanders replied that he had several.

"Then keep 'em loaded," Raider said. "An' don't be 'fraid t' use 'em if the California Kid rides in."

"Four days," Sanders said.

And all they could do was wait.

Four days and nothing had happened.

The Green Sands Ranch felt like the most peaceful place on earth. The sky was clear overhead, the days were warm and the nights were cool. The day of the election had crept up on them and Johnny Sonora was nowhere in sight.

Sanders had chosen not to go back into town to state his case to the voters. The local newspaper had endorsed Franklin Jenkins for mayor, so there didn't seem to be much hope for Sanders. He had been locked in his study the whole time, probably preparing a concession speech.

Raider sat on the porch with his feet propped up. He wondered why Sanders didn't go into town to vote for himself. Was he really going to give up so easily?

"Excuse me, sir."

Dennison was standing behind him. He hadn't even heard the butler come up. Dennison and Tillie had been good to Raider over the last four days, fetching him anything he wanted.

"I was wondering if you'll be eating breakfast this morning," Dennison said. "Should I prepare you a tray?"

Raider nodded. "Where's your boss?"

"Still in the study, sir."

"And the missus?"

"In her room," Dennison replied. "I trust all is well with you, sir?"

Raider saw that the man was sweating bullets off his forehead. "You okay, Dennison?"

"I'm afraid all of this has got me quite unnerved, sir."

Raider looked back out toward the plain. "I reckon it has. But I think the worst might be over now."

"I'll get your breakfast."

Raider thanked him.

After the big man had eaten, Dennison took the tray back to the kitchen.

Raider strolled down to the barn, checking with his sentries. Everything looked calm. The men at the house were having to fight the urge to take a siesta. Raider told them all to stay steady. Sometimes the ground opened up when you least expected it.

But Raider really didn't believe it himself. Sonora hadn't struck and since the day of the election had begun, there was nothing the gunfighter could do to disrupt the voters. And it didn't make sense that the California Kid would try to start trouble after the election.

Sanders came out on the porch after Raider had sat down again. "I'm going into town to cast my vote," the rancher said. "I don't care if everybody in the world tries to kill me. It's my right."

Raider started to get up. "I'll go with you."

Sanders waved him off. "No, I'm going alone. I've got to be a man about this. You stay here and take care of Ellen."

Raider tried to argue him out of it, but Sanders was set. He mounted a big gray gelding and rode off toward Stockton to cast his ballot. Raider worried all day about him, until he rode in again that afternoon.

"No problems?" Raider asked.

Sanders smiled. "No. And by God, I think I have a chance. Several people in town said they were going to vote for me. I could win this thing."

But he didn't. Only they didn't find out till later that night, when Sanders's sentries intercepted the rider. He said he had a message for John Sanders, so they brought the rider straight to the house.

"Confound it!" Sanders cried. "It's almost midnight. Why the devil did you wake me up?"

Raider was standing next to the rancher. He too had been sleeping when the men knocked on the door. They said they found somebody trespassing.

"Ain't done it!" the rider said. "I brought a message for Mr. John Sanders. Ain't s'posed to give it to nobody but him."

Sanders bristled. "I'm waiting."

"Beggin' your pardon," the messenger said. "But you lost the election, Mr. Sanders."

"How many more votes did Jenkins have?" the rancher asked.

"Two hundred, sir. I'm sorry."

Sanders turned back toward the house. "Let him go. I've heard what he came to tell me."

"Wait a minute," the rider said. "I got more."

Sanders looked over his shoulder. "Make it quick."

The man shrugged off his captors. "Give me room, boys."

Raider pointed a finger at the rider. "You heard the man. Let's have it."

"Well, there's a letter here from Mr. Jenkins."

He held out an envelope.

Sanders snatched the message from his hand. Raider held up an oil lamp while he read the message. It was a high-toned letter from the winning candidate. Said that Sanders had waged a clean campaign, that Jenkins was proud to have had such an honorable man running against him.

Sanders laughed a little. "He's taking the high road."

Raider nodded, having read the letter over his shoulder. "Reckon he didn't have nothin' t' do with that other stuff after all."

"That's not all," the rider said.

Sanders exhaled impatiently. "There's more?"

"He wants you to serve as deputy mayor," the man said. "I'm supposed to take your answer back with me."

"Deputy mayor," Raider offered. "Not bad."

Sanders thought it over. "I suppose it's better than losing. Look here, man, what if I accept his offer?"

"Then there's gonna be a big to-do in town tomorrow. A big meetin'. Gonna be food and drink. Ever'body's welcome. Mr. Jenkins wants to start things right. And he figgers he don't want to keep tanglin' with you, Mr. Sanders. Thinks y'all ought to work together."

Raider leaned forward, anticipating another message. "Go on, honcho."

"Well, that's all," the messenger said. "Can I go now?"

Sanders gestured to his men. "Make sure he goes back to town. Escort him there if you have to."

When they were all gone, Sanders turned to Raider. "Do you think this could be some sort of trap?"

"It don't sound like it," Raider replied, his brow fretted. "Why would Jenkins come after you now? He won the election."

"I want you there with me," Sanders said. "In case something goes wrong."

"I won't be far, Sanders."

Raider figured everything would be all right after the big party in town. Then he could leave the case behind him. Hell, there hadn't been much of a case at all. Nothing that would make an interesting report.

"I'm going back to bed," the rancher grumbled. "I'll see you in the morning."

Raider lingered on the porch by himself. He saw a shooting star as it streaked across the sky. He wondered if it was a sign of good luck.

Somewhere in the moonless night, he heard a single coyote howling, a far, lonely cry that echoed through the hills, calling to mind more troubled times when things had not gone his way.

CHAPTER SEVENTEEN

The day could not have been better for a celebration. The household of John Sanders had caught the spirit of the occasion, buzzing about as everyone prepared to go into Stockton. The loss of the election was tempered by the new position that Sanders would hold. Raider wasn't sure what a deputy mayor did for a living, but he figured it didn't matter. Everybody was happy.

Raider sat on the front porch, clad in creased black trousers, a white shirt and a ribbon tie. His Stetson had been dusted and blocked. He could thank Tillie for that. She had even shined his boots for him. He felt like a kid on the way to church.

He heard Mrs. Sanders calling for Dennison inside the house. They were all going to town in the coach when they were ready. Raider hoped the ceremony was short and sweet. He didn't want to listen to speeches all day.

Maybe there would be liquor at the party. Or women. Why not take a chance? Hell, the case was over. Or was it?

Johnny Sonora, alias the California Kid, was still in Manteca. He had worked his way south and if he wasn't just blowing smoke, he would probably return to Stockton. Raider shook it off. He didn't have to think about the kid anymore. He had reported his findings to Sanders, which was the only reason he had been hired. It was time to wrap it up.

The front door of the ranch house swung open. Tillie came out dressed in her Sunday finest. She plopped angrily into the other chair.

"Trouble?" Raider asked.

Tillie scowled at him. "Dat woman gonna drive us all loco. She cain't make up her mind 'bout nuthin'."

He smiled at her. "You sure look pretty, Tillie. I never realized you was so young."

She waved him off, acting coy. "Oh, you go on."

"Is the boss ready?"

"Mr. Sanders been ready for a hour. It's dat woman what's causin' all de ruckus. He ain' gonna git rid of her, is he?"

Raider chortled, looking away. "I can't say, Tillie. But I reckon things are gonna be fine from here on out."

"Uh-huh!"

"Tillie!" Mrs. Sanders called from inside.

The black woman shook her head. "I ain' missin' dis for nuthin'. She better be—"

"Tillie!"

A groan from deep inside her. Then, "I'se comin', Miz Ellen!" She stomped off into the house.

Dennison came through the door before Tillie could close it.

Raider looked back at the butler. "You about ready?"

Dennison was pale. Sweat streamed off his forehead. His hands trembled a little. He looked sick.

"I'm not going to the ceremony," Dennison said. "I'm rather under the weather. And madam is being very difficult this morning."

"Why you think I'm sittin' out here?"

Dennison wiped his face with a cloth. "I can't say that I blame you, sir. Will you be attending the festivities?"

Raider nodded. "That's why I got this outfit on."

"Can I expect you back here this evening?"

The big man nodded. "Yeah, I'm gonna overstay my welcome one more night. Hope I ain't been too much trouble t' y'all."

Dennison smiled weakly. "On the contrary, sir. I've rather enjoyed attending you. You aren't very demanding."

Raider offered his hand. "Shake on it, Dennison."

The butler's hand was clammy.

"You sure you're okay, Dennison? I could whip up some Injun brew if you want it. Cure what ails you."

"I'm sure I'll be fine," the man replied. "I just need some rest. With all the disturbances lately, I've had a few sleepless nights."

"Just take care o' that boss o' yours," Raider offered. "He ain't a bad sort when you come right down to it."

"Quite. I'll see you this evening, sir. I hope you have a good time at the big celebration. I know I'm going to regret missing it, but I need to take to a sick bed for a while."

"Dennison!" It was the voice of Mrs. Sanders.

"The harpy calls," the butler said. "Excuse me, sir."

He went back into the house.

Raider shook his head. He was glad that he would be leaving Green Sands. What the hell kind of name was that for a ranch anyway?

His eyes peered toward the horizon, where a single rider stirred dust. The horse was headed for Stockton. There would be a lot of people in town today. Raider had to wonder if the California Kid would be one of them.

By late afternoon, Raider was tired and a little drunk. Not that he hadn't enjoyed himself at the big whing-ding. The streets of Stockton were crowded with fine citizens who also enjoyed the food and drink. And so far there hadn't been any speeches or any trouble.

It was like a Sunday picnic, only there weren't any tablecloths spread on the ground. Everything was served in front of the saloon or the general store, which made for long lines and waiting time. Raider had avoided all the lines by eating with Sanders and his entourage.

He had stuck by the rancher most of the day, watching the crowd for any sign of Johnny Sonora. Why the hell did he think the kid would come into Stockton? Surely word of the big celebration had gotten to Manteca. Hell, there were cowboys from all directions, lapping up the free beer and roast beef. But there wasn't a blond head among them.

Raider had taken several turns through the gathering to make sure the California Kid wasn't disguised. On one pass, he had come across a black-haired woman who told him how to get to her place. She only charged five dollars, which wasn't a bad rate at all. Raider figured he could get his stuff at the ranch and then sneak back into town. He'd have to send a wire to Wagner to tell him that he was ready for another case. He hoped they would send him east, maybe back to Texas or New Mexico. He didn't really care about working in California any more.

As the approaching dusk turned the sky dark blue, Raider saw torches going up over the same platform where the candidates had spoken a few weeks before. Jenkins and Sanders ascended the platform, raising their hands together. The crowd cheered and called for Jenkins to make a speech.

"As you all know," the new mayor started, "I was chosen by you to lead this great town of Stockton—"

More cheers.

Raider was at the rear of the group that stood in front of the platform. He started to work his way toward Jenkins and Sanders. He wanted to be right next to them, to watch the spectators at the head of the crowd.

"—and if something was to happen to me—"

"God forbid, Franklin!"

"You're young and strong, Jenkins!"

"—my duties will be discharged by this man right here. The new deputy mayor of Stockton. Mister John Sanders!"

The light tapping of applause rose over the crowd.

"Say somethin', Sanders!"

"Yeah, speak up!"

Raider was almost to the platform.

Sanders lifted his hands. "The only thing I have to say is that I thank you all for this honor. If I—"

"John!"

A woman had screamed for Sanders.

Raider stopped and turned to look.

"John, please. John!"

It was Mrs. Sanders. She was coming from the side, trying to get through the crowd to the platform. What the hell was she trying to do? Embarrass her husband?

Sanders glanced nervously over his shoulder. He turned back to the audience, pretending that he had not heard her. But the spectators knew she was there. They were all straining to get a glimpse of her.

"Heard she was foolin' around with somebody," a man said.

"For shame!" a woman rejoined.

"John!" She shoved someone out of her way. "Please, let me through."

Raider tried to get to her but she was already climbing the steps to the platform. The stupid bitch. She was going to make the new deputy mayor look like a fool. Was she just drunk? Or was this part of another scheme?

Sanders held out his hand to her. "My wife, ladies and gentlemen. Mrs. Ellen Sanders."

A smattering of faint applause.

Raider felt his heart thumping. Something was wrong. He could see it in the woman's eyes as she threw her arms around Sanders.

"John, please, you've got to—"

Ellen Sanders swung in front of her husband just as the rifle went off. The slug ripped into her body, causing her to buckle. Sanders tried to catch her but he tripped and went down with her. The rifle exploded again, missing both of them.

Franklin Jenkins dived from the platform into the crowd. Everyone was in a panic, screaming, trying to escape the rifle. Even though the third shot did not come, the spectators still scattered into shops and alleys.

Raider jumped onto the stage, bending over Sanders and his wife. "Let me see her."

Sanders rolled off her, gaping at the blood.

The slug had hit her in the side. It might not be fatal. Raider saw that her blue eyes were still open. Her lips parted in an effort to speak.

"Blond—kid—talking to—to—"

Raider felt his chest tightening. "Where? Where did you see the blond kid? Who was he talkin' to?"

She pointed weakly toward the hotel across the street.

Raider looked up, studying the angle. The shot could've come from the roof of the hotel. Some smoke hung in the air above the structure.

"Honey, can you tell me—"

But she was out cold. Her chest was still moving so she was alive. Maybe she could tell him later.

"Get a doctor," the big man said to Sanders.

The rancher was staring at his wife. "She's dead. Dead!"

Raider slapped him across the face. "No, she's alive. And she might stay that way if you get a doctor."

A young man climbed onto the platform. "I'm Doc Morris."

Raider gestured to Mrs. Sanders. "She's been hit in the side. I think it went all the way through her."

The doctor knelt down to attend the wound.

Raider started off the platform.

"Where are you going?" Sanders called.

"In back o' the hotel."

He hoped he could still catch the man who had taken the rifle shot at Sanders. Or was the bullet meant for Jenkins, the new mayor? No, Mrs. Sanders had seen the kid, had somehow found out that he was going to try to kill her husband. But why?

Raider stopped at the alley that led to the rear entrance of the hotel. He reached into his boot and pulled out his Colt. Sanders had asked him not to wear a sidearm that day, so the big man had opted to store the weapon in his boot. He lifted the gun and thumbed back the hammer.

The alleyway was deserted. Raider ran between the buildings, bursting around the back corner of the hotel. He didn't even have to climb to the roof. He saw where the horse had been waiting. A trail of dust led to the south, toward Manteca. Johnny Sonora had hit quickly and then hightailed it away.

Raider knew what he had to do. Find a fast horse and ride south. Somehow he felt responsible for the ambush. He should have gone after the kid in the first place. Best not to think about his mistakes. Just make sure he got the job done right this time.

CHAPTER EIGHTEEN

Raider couldn't find hide nor hair of Johnny Sonora. The damned California Kid had simply vanished. A livery man in Manteca had sold Sonora a horse the same day that Mrs. Sanders had been shot. Sonora hadn't been seen since then.

So Raider rode in a big circle back to Stockton. He looked for signs of the California Kid but there was no way to pick up a trail. When he hit town later that night, he tried to follow the trail that led away from the rear of the hotel. But it was no use. The tracks ended on a rocky stretch about two miles south of the town line. Raider couldn't follow him in the dark.

He rode into Stockton again, tying his mount in front of the sheriff's office. The lights were still burning over the lawman's desk. Sheriff Calderwood gaped up at the big man when Raider pushed into the dim glow.

"Whatta you know about all this?" Calderwood asked.

Raider sat down in the wooden chair. "It's Sonora. He was after John Sanders. I still don't know why he waited until after the election."

Calderwood grimaced. "Sonora?"

"The California Kid."

"Oh."

Raider exhaled dejectedly. "I should've taken him when I had the chance. But hell, I couldn't just kill him, not without a reason."

"You got one now," the sheriff rejoined. "If he's the one who shot Mrs. Sanders."

"Who else?"

Calderwood shook his head. "I ain't got one notion."

Raider asked for whiskey.

The sheriff joined him in a snort.

"Why would Sonora want to kill Sanders?" Calderwood asked.

Raider shrugged. "Well, I was thinkin' that your boy Jenkins was b'hind it. But hell, he couldn't be the one. Not the way he was treatin' Sanders today. They're buddies now."

The sheriff's brow wrinkled. "I ain't one to bad-mouth Franklin Jenkins, but couldn't he have hired somebody to shoot Sanders?"

"It's possible," Raider replied. "But use your skull. Jenkins is a politician. If he wanted Sanders out of the picture, he wouldn't have done it right after the election. He would've done it before."

"Makes sense."

"It all fit before the election. Sanders hired me to find out why Johnny Sonora was goin' by his old name."

Calderwood gawked at him. "What the hell you say?"

"Sanders used to be the California Kid," Raider offered. "Back b'fore the war. Had hisself somethin' of a reputation. But he wanted to put all that b'hind him. Then this kid turns up. Sanders thought it was Jenkins who brought the kid back. Figgered to ruin Sanders by revealin' his old business. Only that's all bullshit now."

"Maybe this kid is actin' on his own," the sheriff said. "He might have his own reasons for killin' Sanders."

Raider eyed the lawman. "What're you gonna do 'bout this, Calderwood?"

The sheriff shrugged. "I got a posse workin'. We're gonna start out at daybreak. You wanna come along?"

"No. I gotta get back out t' the ranch, t' make sure Sanders is all right. He let some of his men go this mornin'. Figgered we didn't need that much protection."

"I'll swing by the day after tomorrow and see Sanders," the sheriff volunteered.

Raider suddenly remembered the woman. "Has Ellen Sanders been talkin'?"

Calderwood shook his head. "Can't say as I really know. They took her back to the ranch. The doc thinks she's gonna live. Why?"

"She said she saw the kid in town afore she was shot," the big man replied. "Said she saw Sonora with somebody."

"Who?"

"Hell, sheriff, that's what I'd like t' know. That's what I been lookin' for all along."

Sheriff Calderwood reached for a rifle that lay crossways on his desk. "Don't worry, Pinkerton. If this kid is still in the territory, we'll find him. He won't get by us."

Raider nodded and excused himself. He appreciated the sheriff's efforts and optimism but he knew better. Sonora wasn't the kind of man to sit still for two days while some tinhorn lawman got a posse together. No, the sheriff's ploy was strictly show for the citizens of Stockton. He was never going to catch the California Kid.

Raider figured to rest the stallion when he got back to Green Sands. The animal had served him well and he didn't want to ride it into the ground. It deserved a warm stall and an oat bag.

He wished he knew what he was going to do after he took care of the black. His best bet was to talk to Mrs. Sanders. She had the key. If she identified the man she had seen with Sonora, then Raider's search would be over.

The ranch house was dark as Raider approached on the stallion. No sentries at the door or on top of the roof. No guards in the barn. Had Sanders been foolish enough to leave the house unprotected?

Raider held his Colt in hand as he stepped up onto the front porch. He tried the door, which was open. Easing into the blackness, he listened, wondering if Sonora had already come to Green Sands.

Something flashed in front of the big man.

He aimed the Colt at the ball of light.

A candle burned to life, illuminating the room. He had almost shot Dennison, the butler. He pointed the Colt at the floor.

"You scared the livin' shit outta me, Dennison."

The butler glared at him. "It is rather late, sir. I heard some-one coming in and I came to investigate."

Raider nodded. "Thanks. How's ever'thin' 'round here? Is Mrs. Sanders still with us?"

"She's doing quite well, sir. She's sleeping now. As is Mr. Sanders."

Raider pointed to the stairs. "I wanna look in on Mrs. Sanders. See if she's talkin' yet."

"I wouldn't advise that, sir. She has been shot, after all. Very disquieting to me. I had thought all of this was over."

Dennison looked pale and sweaty.

Raider started for the stairs, figuring his investigation should prevail over the orders of a manservant. "I gotta see if she's awake, Dennison. An' if she ain't, I'm gonna sit there till she opens her eyes."

He thought the butler was going to protest, but instead, Dennison decided to be helpful. "Shall I bring you some coffee, sir?"

"That's more like it," Raider said.

He stepped slowly on the stairs, heading for the bedchamber of Ellen Sanders.

Mrs. Sanders looked pitiful lying on her bed. A low-burning lamp sat on the nightstand next to her. She was bandaged from hip to shoulder. Her face had turned white. She hadn't deserved a bullet, not since she had saved her husband's life.

Her eyes were closed. Raider sat down next to the bed. He reached out and took her hand.

Ellen Sanders opened her eyes. "Dennison—" she muttered.

Raider patted the back of her hand. "No, it's me, Raider. Can you talk? Can you tell me who you saw with the kid before you got shot?"

She closed her eyes. "Dennison—"

"No, it's me, Raider, I—"

The butler came into the room with a tray. "Your coffee, sir."

"She's askin' for you," Raider said.

Dennison touched his hand to her forehead. "Still feverish. Here, the doctor left a powder. I'll have to mix it with water. It's supposed to make her sleep."

The big man nodded. "Pour me some o' that coffee while you're at it."

Raider sipped from a steaming cup as Dennison prepared the

powder. It reminded him of his old partner, Doc Weatherbee. One of Doc's covers had been that of apothecary. Doc was always making potions. Maybe he could have figured out this damned case by now.

Dennison lifted the glass to Mrs. Sanders's mouth. "Come on, madam. Drink for me. That's it."

She opened her eyes while she was drinking. She started to cough and gag. Raider touched her hand again. He knew how it felt to get wounded by a piece of lead.

"Dennison—" She drifted off again, breathing heavily.

"Yes, madam, I'm right here. Let me dry some of this water that you've spilled. We must keep you nice and neat."

Raider drained the last of the coffee. "Not bad. How 'bout another cup? I wanna stay awake for a while."

"As you wish, sir."

Raider started on a new cup. "Hell, Dennison, I don't know what these folks would do without you."

"They'd probably hire someone else," the butler replied. "I'm little more than an ornament to them."

Raider tried to ignore the butler's bitter tone. "Aw, I wouldn't say that, Dennison. They depend on you. By the way, I wanna talk t' Mr. Sanders as soon as he wakes up."

"As you wish, sir."

"You think Tillie could rustle up some grub?"

"Tillie went to visit her sister in Sacramento," Dennison replied. "But I would be happy to bring you some cold meat and some bread."

Raider nodded. "That's plenty."

The butler hesitated, staring at Mrs. Sanders. Sweat poured off him. He still looked sick.

"You all right?" Raider asked.

Dennison sighed. "I don't know how much more of this I can stand, sir. Things were never this way in England."

"Maybe you oughta go back there."

A slight smile on the man's lips. "Precisely, sir, as soon as I've found my fortune here in the states."

He started to go.

Raider told him to wait a minute. "Dennison, you got any notions 'bout who shot Mrs. Sanders?"

"No, sir. None whatsoever. I'm just glad I wasn't there to witness it."

Raider yawned. "Yeah, I reckon. I better finish this coffee. I'm startin' t' drag here."

He lifted the cup to his lips. It tasted good going down. A little sweet, like Dennison had flavored it with honey. He leaned back in the chair. Damn it all, his head felt like it was about to float off his neck.

Mrs. Sanders stirred a little. She called the butler's name in her sleep. Raider reached forward again to touch her hand, but this time he found himself on the floor. His arms and legs wouldn't move.

Sleep. He needed sleep. Lots of it.

He wanted to call for Dennison. It wasn't right to go to sleep on the floor. He had to get to his bed.

His body felt like it was going to start floating. That was it, he could float to his bed. If somebody would just help him.

Mrs. Sanders called in her sleep again. "Dennison—"

For an instant before he passed out, Raider knew the truth.

But he couldn't do a thing about it.

His arms were lying limply by his side. He couldn't even reach his Colt. His eyes closed and he slept for a long time. When he woke up again, he would be able to figure it the right way. But by then it would be too late.

CHAPTER NINETEEN

Raider wanted the grizzly bear to get off his head. It felt like claws sinking into his skull. He opened his eyes but saw only darkness. Something was sticking him in the head. He tried to move but he was suddenly nauseous. Nothing came up when he attempted to heave. He just groaned.

"The fuzz will wear off after a while," a voice said.

Raider thought he knew the man, but he wasn't sure. "What fuzz?" he heard himself saying to the darkness.

"The fuzz in your head, the fuzz on your tongue. It wore off for me anyway. Took half a day and a couple of gallons of water."

"Sanders?"

The rancher sighed. "You were drugged, Raider. Just like me. Welcome to the cellar. I thought I was dreaming when I first woke up. But I wasn't."

Some of it came back to him. He didn't yet remember drinking the coffee that had knocked him out. But he did recall the investigation, all the way up to the time Mrs. Sanders was shot.

"Where the hell are we?" he asked the rancher.

"In the cellar of my house. You can see a little bit better during the day. Some light trickles in."

Raider figured he had better try to sit up. His head whirled when he moved, but he managed to lean against the wall. He waited for the cobwebs to go away. It was going to take a while.

"You want some water?" Sanders asked.

"Yeah. Where are you?"

"Just reach your hand out a few feet to your left. I'm holding the dipper by the bowl. You can find the handle."

It worked well enough. Raider spilled a little but managed to get the dipper to his lips. The water made him nauseous for a moment, until he broke a sweat. He drank some more.

"I figure he used the same stuff that the doctor gave my wife for pain," the rancher offered. "I was having some brandy; the next thing I know, I'm in this cellar chained to the wall."

Raider exhaled. "I was drinkin' coffee. An' you're prob'ly right. Dennison drugged us with the powder the doctor gave your wife."

"Why the devil would he drug us?" Sanders said.

"Mebbe he didn't have much choice. Mebbe the kid has got a gun in his ear. It stands to reason that Sonora is here. Hell, I couldn't find him anywhere else."

Sanders made a whistling sound. "I never thought of that. Hell, I give up. I can't understand why this kid would want to hurt me and my wife. What did I ever do to him?"

Raider closed his eyes, wishing his headache would go away. "Sometimes it don't take much t' make a man hate."

"I wonder what they plan to do with us?"

Raider took a deep breath. "I ain't too worried 'bout that. How long was I sleepin'?"

"Well, they brought you in last night and you slept all through the day. It's after nine o'clock now. I heard the clock chime in the kitchen."

"You said *they* brought me."

Sanders sighed. "Yes, two of them. They wore hoods over their heads so I couldn't see who they were."

"They been feedin' you?"

"No," the rancher said. "They just left me this bucket and dipper. I guess that means they're going to kill us."

"Mebbe. I'll have to study on it some."

Sanders stuttered for a moment. "You—I mean, you don't really think you can get us out of this mess?"

"Just hush for now. An' give me some more water."

The dipper changed hands more smoothly the second time. Raider drank it all down. He felt sick for a while but the sweat came back. Damn. The kid had forced Dennison to drug them. Sonora had probably come back when everybody was gone, after he had tried to kill Sanders. Then he had made the butler dismiss the remaining hired hands.

Raider had to kick himself. Sonora had run to the last place anybody would have looked for him. And he was letting Dennison take care of Ellen Sanders. Maybe there had been a plan and the lady had gotten cold feet at the last minute, couldn't bear to watch her husband die on the platform. It was all so damned confusing.

"Pinkerton, could you—"

"Hush up," the big man said. "I gotta sleep."

"But I just want to say that there's a big reward for you if I get out of this alive."

Raider tried to laugh. "You won't owe me a thing, Sanders. I gotta save my ass too. I reckon it all hangs on what they want from us."

"That's right," Sanders rejoined, "at least they haven't killed us yet. But they'll have to move soon. I'm an important man. If I don't turn up for a couple of days, I'm going to be missed. And the doctor will be coming back to see Ellen."

"Then hush up an' let me sleep!"

"Anything you say, Raider. Anything you say."

"Raider?"

The big man from Arkansas opened his eyes. He could see the figure of John Sanders, formerly the California Kid, sitting across from him. It was morning and sunlight spilled into the basement.

"I thought I should wake you."

Raider sat up. He grabbed the chain that held him captive, following the links to the end. The chain had been forged to a thick eye-hook that was buried in the stone wall. Raider tried to yank the hook out of the wall.

"It's in there tight," Sanders said. "I built it myself. You can't budge it with your own strength."

Raider looked closer at the hook. "What'd you fasten it to when you put it in the wall?"

Sanders shrugged. "Nothing really. There's just a tee-shaped piece of metal and some stones."

Raider reached into his boot, grabbing his hunting knife.

Sanders chortled. "Won't be able to cut through these chains with that blade, Pinkerton."

"I ain't cuttin' the chains."

He started to chip away at the plaster around the eye hook.

Sanders straightened a little. "You think you can cut into the wall?"

"Mebbe. If I get it dug out, there ain't nothin' holdin' this hook."

Sanders pointed to the other side of the cellar. "If you can get free, Raider, there's an old Navy Colt in that tool chest over there. I keep it down here for emergencies. Had to shoot a snake once."

Raider stopped for a moment.

Sanders gaped at him. "What the—"

Raider raised a hand. He could hear footsteps above him. The others had risen for the day. Who the hell were they? "Two of 'em," he said in a low voice. "I gotta get outta here an' finish this. Too many people have been hurt."

He started chipping at the wall again.

"What if they come to get us now?" Sanders said.

Raider chipped a little faster.

When the big man pulled the eye-hook out of the wall, Sanders almost let out a cheer. Raider told him to keep quiet and point the way to the old Colt. Sanders directed him to the tool chest.

The Colt was a percussion job. Raider loaded it carefully. With the kid on the premises, he couldn't afford a misfire. He wished he had time to study the weapon, to shoot with it a couple of times. He'd just have to take his chances on the first shot, make the adjustment if he got off a second round.

Raider hefted the Colt in his hand and then started for the stairs that led out of the cellar.

Sanders gasped. "Listen. They're coming."

Raider heard footsteps above him. He quickly pressed himself against the wall, waiting for someone to come down into the cellar.

•   •   •

When the hooded figure moved past him, Raider put the barrel of the Colt against the man's head. "Hold real steady."

The hooded man didn't move.

Raider reached for the man's sidearm, a new Colt Peacemaker. "You can take off the hood, kid. I recognize your gun."

Johnny Sonora took off the hood. He smiled good-naturedly at Raider. "Reckon I never could fool you, Ray."

The big man from Arkansas pinned him to the wall, holding the pistol on the tip of his nose. "You got keys to these handcuffs?"

"Hey, no need for the rough stuff. I'll unlock you, Ray. I got nothin' agin' you."

He pushed the kid toward John Sanders. "Unlock him. An' then Sanders can unlock me."

Sonora obeyed without hesitation. "Like I said, Ray, no reason we can't be on the same side." He turned the key in the lock on Sanders's wrists.

Raider held both Colts on Sonora as Sanders freed himself from the manacles. "Here, Sanders, take the Navy. We're gonna have some fun with the California Kid. Hey, Johnny, did you know this was the man who used t' have your name?"

Sonora eyed the rancher. "Yeah, I know. Hell, he don't look so tough to me."

Raider nodded. "Yeah, he got old. But you won't live so long, kid. You'll prob'ly swing from a rope."

"Aw, I ain't done nothin' wrong."

"You tried to kill my wife!" Sanders cried, thumbing back the hammer of the Navy. "Now I ought to kill you!"

Raider stepped between the kid and the rancher. "Not yet, Sanders. I wanna hear him out. He's got a lotta talkin' t' do."

Sonora's smile disappeared. "Give it up, Ray. You ain't never gonna take me outta here alive."

"Then I'll take you out dead," the big man replied. "Who hired you, Sonora? Why'd you come to Stockton? Why'd you try to kill Sanders?"

The kid shrugged. "How you know it was me that tried to kill the old man? Coulda been somebody else."

Raider growled at the outlaw. "Don't play pussyfoot with me, Sonora. You came to Stockton for a reason."

"Yeah? Says who?"

"In the saloon, before you knew I was a Pinkerton, you told

me that you planned to find your fortune in Stockton. That some-thin' big was gonna happen for you. What'd you hope to get from Sanders?"

"You got it all wrong, Ray," the kid rejoined. "I never wanted nothin' from this old boy. And I didn't shoot the woman neither. None of it was my plan. I just used the old man's name, like I was paid to do. Killed a few people so I'd have a reputation. I wasn't nothin' before then. Just a cowhand with a fast gun."

"Why'd you take my old name?" Sanders cried. "Tell me or I'll shoot you right now!"

Sonora nodded toward the stairs. "Why don't you ask the man standin' behind you with the shotgun?"

Raider chortled. "That's an old one, Sonora. Now s'pose you tell me the truth."

"He is telling the truth." The voice had come from behind them.

Raider started to turn.

"Don't. I'll give you both barrels straight in the back. Drop those weapons this instant."

Sanders dropped the Navy and looked over his shoulder. "Dennison! But, you could save us!"

Raider tossed the kid's Peacemaker on the floor. "Can it, Sanders. It won't do any good."

The butler motioned with the shotgun. "Chain them up again," he told the kid. "Tie the big one to the rafter."

"Gonna have to kill us quick," Raider offered.

"I will," Dennison replied. "But first, I want to tell you how I staged the whole thing. You do want to know, don't you, Pinker-ton?"

Raider said he'd just love to hear all about it.

CHAPTER TWENTY

When Raider and Sanders were chained again, Dennison lowered the barrel of the scattergun. "You never had a clue that it was me behind the kid, did you, Mr. Pinkerton?"

Raider just stayed quiet, wondering how the hell he was going to get out of this mess. Let Dennison say his piece. There might be something useful in his words.

The butler began to pace as much as the basement would let him. "You know, Sanders, being your valet allowed me to listen in on many of your private conversations. Do you remember saying that you had many women in your past? Lots of women?"

Sanders shrugged. "Yes, but—"

"San Francisco," Dennison went on, "a woman named Belle. Do you remember her? She had dark hair and a kind face."

Sanders lowered his eyes. "Yes, I remember Belle. I loved her. I really did. I hated to leave her, but I had to go off to war."

The butler chortled cynically. "She was a whore, but she was my mother. I loved her as well, but I didn't leave her like you did."

The rancher looked up. "Are you my—"

"Son?" Dennison laughed loudly. "No, I'm not your son. I was a young boy when you came around to see my mother. I always stayed in the back room. But I could hear you making promises that you would never keep."

"Seems you like t' listen t' other people's private talk," Raider said sarcastically. "You ain't nothin' but a nosy ol' lady."

Dennison smiled. "Yes, but I'm a nosy old lady with a shotgun."

"You can't kill us," Sanders said. "I'll give you whatever you want. But please, let us go."

The butler shook his head. "I can't. The big man here would never let me rest. Would you, Raider?"

"Well, you did kinda kidnap us, Dennison. An' far as I know, that's agin' the law. But hell, let's don't go on 'bout it. I wanna know why you hired this boy t' pretend he was the California Kid."

"It was all for my mother," the man replied. "Yes, she was a whore. And she whored for fancy gentlemen. That's how I got to England. She was the kept woman of some count for a while. I learned how to be a butler."

Raider whistled. "And you just come on back here t' get even with John Sanders because he left your ma?"

Dennison shrugged. "No, not really, not at first. Coincidence played a big part. I came home to San Francisco. I had a little money, so I lived like a gentleman for a while. When my funds ran low, I had to look for work. You can imagine my delight when I saw an advertisement asking for a man's man. I had forgotten about Johnny Sonora, the famous California Kid that my mother had always told me about."

"Belle," Sanders said. "Is she alive?"

"No," Dennison replied. "She's not."

Raider glared at the butler. "Well, if you didn't know Sanders was the California Kid, then how'd you find out?"

"That old trunk full of artifacts," Dennison replied. "I went through it carefully, replacing everything the way it had been before. You can imagine how lucky I felt. Here was the man who deserted my mother. And here was my chance to get even with him."

"So you cooked up the scheme to bring back the California Kid," Raider offered. "To discredit Sanders so he'd lose the election."

Dennison shook his head. "Not even close. I didn't care one

way or the other about the election. No, I just wanted the kid here to have a reputation. I wanted everyone to know that Johnny Sonora was operating in the area. That way when Sanders was killed, I could implement the second half of my plan."

Sanders gaped at his former manservant. "What the hell did you have in mind, Dennison?"

"Simple. After you're killed, there's a big investigation. The kid would be suspected, until I told everyone that he was at the ranch with me when Sanders was shot. You see, I planned to uncover the trunk that linked the two California Kids. Johnny here was going to claim he was Johnny Sonora junior and therefore entitled to a portion of the Sanders fortune."

Raider glanced at the kid. "So you wanted t' take one little potshot for your inheritance. Thought you wasn't one t' shoot a innocent man, kid."

Sonora shrugged and laughed. "It weren't me that shot the woman. Like the man said, I was here most of the time. I was supposed to say that I had come to see my father."

Sanders scowled at Dennison. "You shot Ellen!"

Dennison smiled. "Yes, but the bullet was meant for you. And you still have to die, Sanders. But how? I'll have to figure out a way that makes it appear that you were killed by someone other than me. But that shouldn't be too hard."

"Don't it bother you to kill a man?" Raider asked.

"I'm not killing a man," the butler replied. "I'm killing the California Kid. And when his son assumes the throne, I'll be right there calling all the shots. Johnny Sonora junior will see the error of his ways and decide to live a good life. Won't you, Johnny?"

The kid grimaced. "I reckon."

Raider's black eyes narrowed. "You won't pull it off, Dennison. You're forgettin' that you have t' get rid o' me too. An' my agency won't take that layin' down. When I turn up missin', this place is gonna be crawlin' with Pinkerton agents."

Dennison frowned. "Admittedly, I will have to be a bit more careful now. But I'm going to get out of this without a scratch. Now, if you'll excuse me, gentlemen, I'm going upstairs."

He turned and started for the stairs.

"I'll kill you with my bare hands!" John Sanders cried. "I'll tear out your heart and crush it!"

But Dennison did not look back.

Johnny Sonora paused at the bottom of the steps, glancing at Raider. "Sorry about this, Ray. You know, if you want me to talk to the man, I'll try to see if there's some way you can get out of this. I mean, all you have to do is go along with it. Would that be so bad?"

Raider shook his head. "You just don't get it, do you, Johnny?"

"Get what?"

"I can't help you, Kid. You dug this hole and you're probably gonna have t' lie in it."

Sonora gestured toward the rafter above the big man. "You're the one who's chained up, Ray. You're the one who don't want out of this. But you can't say that I didn't give you a chance."

The California Kid started up the stairs.

"I'll kill you too!" Sanders cried.

Raider knew it wouldn't do any good to rant. He had to figure a way out of the cellar. One chance was all he needed. A break. It came later that day, when the shooting started upstairs.

Around noontime, somebody knocked on the front door of the ranch house. Raider and Sanders heard the footsteps above them. Boots on the stairs going to the second floor.

Raider looked at the rancher. "The doctor."

"You think he'll notice that I'm not here?"

"Shh."

The doctor was with Mrs. Sanders for an hour before he came downstairs again. He spoke to Dennison, although Raider and Sanders could not hear the exact words. Then he left.

Sanders sighed. "So much for that."

Raider tried to remain calm in the stale air of the cellar. Sanders seemed to be on the verge of panic. The big man couldn't blame him. It looked damned bad. What if Dennison and the kid came downstairs to shoot them like dogs in chains? The butler was pretty clever. Could he really make it look like he hadn't killed them?

"I don't want to die," Sanders said.

"Neither do I, Sanders. But we gotta sit tight while we're still breathin'. Won't do any good t' wail 'bout it."

"I just don't want to die; not like this."

Raider exhaled, closing his eyes. There had to be a way out. He studied on it for a long time, until he heard the first shot. Then he had to wonder if he would be the next one to die.

Sanders looked up when the pistol exploded. "What was that?"

Raider just listened. There was scuffling above them. More shots. He heard voices.

"The sheriff!" he said finally.

Sanders had hope in his face. "You think so?"

More shots.

Someone scuffling up the stairs.

"Ellen!" Sanders cried.

More shots.

Raider heard a thud as somebody dropped down from the second story. Boots on the ground outside, heading for the barn. More shots. He thought he heard the sheriff yelling. Another pistol went off.

He held his breath, listening.

Suddenly things were quiet.

Footsteps approached the cellar door. "Anybody down there?"

Raider yelled back. "That you, Calderwood?"

Boots on the steps. The sheriff came into the basement. He gawked at Raider and Sanders.

"Well don't just stand there," the big man cried. "Get us loose!"

Calderwood shook his head. "I hope you boys can tell me what this is all about."

Raider nodded. "Just set us free. Where's that butler? He should have the key."

"He's lyin' upstairs with a bullet in him," the sheriff replied.

Raider exhaled. "Damn. I wanted him t' stand trial an' hang. Is he dead?"

"As a doornail."

The sheriff started back up the stairs. "I'll get the key."

Sanders gawked after him. "Sheriff, how did you know that Dennison was holding us prisoner?"

Calderwood glanced over his shoulder. "Your wife told the doctor all about it when he came to see her. She pretended to be out until the butler left. Then she was all over the doctor, warnin' him to get out, to come get me. Hell, we met on the road. I was comin' out here anyway to check on your missus. That dead boy upstairs shouldn'ta fought. He wasn't very good with a handgun."

"What about the kid?" Raider asked. "Did you get him?"

Calderwood frowned. "Kid?"

Raider's face went red. "You mean you didn't get Sonora?"

"No. I didn't see him."

"That's b'cause he dropped out the back window an' hightailed it. Get me free, sheriff. I gotta find him."

Calderwood went to look for the key.

Raider shook his head. "The California Kid got away."

"I'm going with you," Sanders offered.

"No. I'll get him."

"I owe him!" the rancher cried. "And nothing is going to stop me from evening the score."

Raider figured he could get the sheriff to restrain Sanders. He didn't need the old boy along to ruin things. Sanders could sure as hell get himself killed if he walked into a stray bullet. Raider knew he was going to have to face the kid head on. They'd finally know which one of them was the fastest.

Footsteps in the stairwell. "I found the key." Calderwood came into the basement. He unlocked Raider first.

The big man didn't waste any time heading upstairs. He had to get his gear ready and then thank Mrs. Sanders for saving his life. She wasn't turning out to be such a bad woman after all.

He rushed past the dead body of Dennison.

When he got to his gear, there was a piece of paper lying on his saddlebags. A message. He unfolded the paper.

See you in Manteca.

It was signed "The California Kid."

CHAPTER TWENTY-ONE

Raider climbed off the black stallion, hitching it to the post in front of the Manteca Inn and Cantina. He saw the sorrel mare that was also tied to the post. It bore the brand of the Green Sands Ranch. Johnny Sonora had stolen it from Sanders's stable.

Raider strode through the swinging doors. There was plenty of light inside, so he didn't have any trouble seeing the California Kid. Johnny smiled and lifted a shot glass, toasting the big man.

"That didn't take long," Sonora said. "Why don't you sit on down here and have a drink with me, Ray?"

"You know I can't do that, Johnny."

The kid frowned. "Aw, I was hopin' you weren't gonna be a hard ass about this, big man."

Raider watched the kid's hands, which were still wrapped around a whiskey bottle. "You coulda kept runnin', Johnny. Why didn't you?"

The kid sighed deeply. "'Cause I knowed you was gonna be chasin' me, Ray. You ain't the kind to give up on somethin'. Sooner or later it's gonna come down to me and you facin' off. Unless I can talk you out of it."

"You can't," Raider replied. "You gotta come back t' Stockton, Johnny. You'll get a fair trial."

"Shee-it," the kid scoffed, "that ain't gonna happen, Ray. I'm the California Kid now. And like it or not, I threw in with that fancy-talkin' butler. He hired me and I did what he said. They got a law agin' stuff like that. Ain't they?"

Raider nodded. "It's called conspiracy. And you could get charged with attemptin' t' kill Mrs. Sanders."

Sonora pointed a finger at him. "Hey, I never shot her. That was ol' Dennison did that."

"You were in town the day she was shot. She saw you talkin' t' the butler. You shoulda killed her while you had the chance."

"I wouldn't let Dennison kill her," Sonora offered. "He wanted to finish her off when the doctor brought her back to the ranch. But I figured we could pay her off. Reckon I was wrong."

"Come back with me, Johnny. Take your chances with a jury. You're young and strong. Prison wouldn't kill you. You'd still have some time left when you got out."

Sonora chortled, shaking his head. "I knew I shouldn'ta throwed in with that fancy-pants. And you know what, Ray? I kinda like you. I wouldn'ta let old Dennison hurt you."

"You're too good, kid. Now, why don't you stand up real slowlike and let me see your sidearm."

Sonora's smile disappeared. "It can't be like that, Ray."

"You want a fair fight?"

The outlaw nodded. "In the street. There's still plenty of light. Fair and square."

"Let's go."

They marched into the tiny dirt street of Manteca. Windows and doors slammed shut in the little village. A few passersby ran for cover. Cracks were left in curtains so curious eyes could watch the showdown.

Raider squared his shoulders to the kid.

Sonora turned himself, standing about ten yards from the big man.

"You want to check your gun?" the kid asked.

Raider shook his head. "You?"

"No."

The big man felt a cold sweat breaking all over him.

Sonora hung his hand by his side. "You draw first, Ray."

Raider's gut was churning. Sweat dripped into his eyes. He went for his Colt, but like before, he never saw the kid's hand move. Johnny Sonora beat him to the punch.

Raider's gun hand went numb. Blood poured from a gash on the back of his hand. He dropped the Colt into the street. His fingers wouldn't work.

Sonora held his Peacemaker steady, walking straight for Raider. "I don't want to kill you, Ray. But like I said, you ain't the kind to quit. I got to finish you."

He saw the hesitation in the kid's eyes. "You coulda shot me just now, Johnny. Only you winged my hand. You don't have it in you t' kill me. I can't shoot back an' I never knowed you t' kill an unarmed man."

Sonora's hand began to tremble. "I got to do it, Ray. I can't go to prison. You know what it's like to want to be free. I can't look out through bars ever'day. I'm sorry."

He thumbed back the hammer of the Peacemaker.

Raider scowled at the kid. "Go on, Sonora. Put one b'tween my eyes. If you got the guts."

"Ray—"

The big man knew he couldn't do it. Sonora started to lower the weapon. But then a rifle exploded and the kid's body buckled. He fell into the street, grabbing his chest. The slug had struck him in the heart.

Raider looked to his left. The shot had come from an alley between the general store and the livery. He saw the man who had fired the shot emerging into the street.

"Sanders!"

The rancher looked down at the body. "I followed you here. I saw that note in your room. It's finished now."

Raider shook his head. "You didn't have t' shoot him. He was about t' give up."

"Looked like he was about to plug you from where I stood, Raider. I thought I was saving your life."

The big man sighed. "It don't matter. Ow—"

"Better have that hand looked at by the doctor."

"As soon as we get the kid back to Stockton."

Until then, his hand would just have to hurt.

The sheriff listened for a long time to the evidence presented by Raider and John Sanders. He had to shake his head a couple of times. It sounded so damned farfetched. But he finally had to believe them.

"Well," Calderwood said at the end of their testimony, "what do you want me to do about all this?"

"Just wanted you t' know," Raider said. "I gotta write a report an' you could do the same if you wanna say anythin' t' my boss."

Calderwood threw out his hands. "What can I say? You tore through this like shit through a chicken, Pinkerton. Probably saved me a lot of grief."

Sanders exhaled defeatedly. "I'll have to resign as deputy mayor."

"Why?" the sheriff replied. "Ever'body has heard about you bein' the California Kid. Nobody holds it agin' you. Jenkins wants you to stay on."

Sanders brightened. "Really?"

Raider started to get up. "If you don't need me, Calderwood, I'm gonna go see the doc."

"May want you to sign some papers later, but you can go for now," the sheriff replied. "Try to stay out of trouble."

"I will, sheriff. I'll do my damnedest."

On the street, a few people pointed at him and whispered. He didn't care. He couldn't wait to get the hell out of Stockton. He decided to send a telegram to the home office before he got his hand tended to.

When the wire was on the way to Chicago, he found the doctor and had him look at the wound. It wasn't serious, the physician told him. He wasn't going to lose his fast-draw abilities. The big Pinkerton could still make a living with his gun.

Raider just nodded, taking the news in stride. He had had enough of killing for a while. He just wanted to take it easy. Forget about a few things. He wouldn't feel like going into action right away again.

Then he got the message from Wagner.

CHAPTER TWENTY-TWO

P. W. Avery stood before the judge, his head hung in sorrow.

Wagner was next to his agent, seated in a chair beside the lawyer. Wagner was pleased with the case as presented by the attorney, but one could never be sure about a local jury. Avery seemed to think that he was going to be convicted.

The judge looked over at the foreman of the jury. "Mr. Foreman, do you have a verdict?"

The foreman nodded.

"Would you please read the verdict to the court?"

"Yes, Judge. We find P. W. Avery guilty on all counts."

A roar erupted from the spectators.

Somebody cried, "They're gonna hang the Pinkerton!"

The judge demanded silence and order.

P. W. Avery slipped back into his chair. "I knew it." He had blanched as white as ash.

Wagner turned to the lawyer. "Petition to get the sentencing delayed."

The attorney stood up. "Your honor, I call for a motion to put off sentencing until an appeal can be filed."

A groan from the audience. The town wanted a hanging. They wanted to see P. W. Avery swing for killing one of their own.

They never took into consideration that the agent had been totally justified in his actions. The jury didn't seem to care, either.

"Motion denied," the judge said. "Mr. P. W. Avery, will rise and face the court."

Avery wobbled on weak legs.

"I hereby sentence you to hang by the neck until dead," the judge said. "So let it be ordered."

Cheering from the spectators.

Avery sat down again.

"Motion to delay execution until appeals can be made for clemency," the lawyer said.

The judge rubbed his chin. "Hangin' will be set for one month from today, sir. Write as many petitions as you can between now and then. Court is adjourned. Take the prisoner into custody."

Two lawmen grabbed Avery.

"I swear I didn't kill that man in cold blood, Mr. Wagner. You got to believe me."

The lawmen started to drag him away.

"I believe you," Wagner called. "And I won't let them hang you, Avery. I promise."

Wagner turned back to the lawyer, who frowned dolefully at him.

"This may take longer than a month, Mr. Wagner."

"Do what you can."

Wagner stormed out of the courthouse. He had two things in mind. A direct appeal to the governor of Nebraska, who could pardon Avery. Or, he could call in Raider. The big man from Arkansas would be able to free Avery all by himself.

The private coach was still with him, so Wagner decided to head for Lincoln, as soon as he got off a wire that requested Raider's presence in Milford, Nebraska.

EPILOGUE

Raider sat on the train to San Francisco, wishing that the journey was already over. It felt funny, coming back to 'Frisco after all that trouble he had seen with John Sanders and the case of the California Kid. The whole thing had happened more than three months ago, but it seemed like a lot longer. Raider had been busy in Nebraska, freeing P. W. Avery from some small-town jail.

The Avery breakout was the first unlawful mission that had ever been authorized by William Wagner. Of course, everything had been straightened out, thanks to Raider. The big man had gone back over Avery's trail, reminding the state authorities what had really happened. The conviction had been overturned and Avery was now a free man.

So here he was, heading back to 'Frisco, summoned by a man named E. B. Chesterton. The message didn't really say what Mr. Chesterton wanted, just that Raider was supposed to report to the Grandview Hotel.

The big man wondered if it had anything to do with John Sanders. After all, Sanders had met him at the Grandview before. And as before, all of Raider's expenses were being paid by the client.

Probably a friend of John Sanders, he thought. He figured the rancher would speak highly of his services. And Raider had not made a big thing out of Sanders killing Johnny Sonora, whose real name had been Henry Ledbetter. It really hadn't mattered. Sonora would have been killed sooner or later. You always met someone faster than you. Raider had found that out when he had faced the California Kid.

Best just to rest up, get back into the swing.

He closed his eyes and slept the rest of the way to San Francisco.

The desk clerk remembered the big man from Arkansas. "Welcome back to the Grandview, sir. Miss Chesterton is waiting for you upstairs."

He handed Raider a key.

"*Miss* Chesterton?"

The clerk nodded. "Yes, she came in yesterday. Said to send you up as soon as you arrived."

Raider frowned. "Okay. If you say so."

He slung his gear over his shoulder and started up the stairs.

The door was open so he didn't have to use his key.

When he entered the room, a woman turned to face him.

"Hello, Raider. It's good to see you again."

Raider gawked at her. "Mrs. Sanders?"

She came toward him, tying a sash around a lacy white robe. "I'm Miss Ellen Chesterton now. I took back my maiden name when John died."

Raider dropped his gear and closed the door behind him. "What'd you do? Kill him?"

She frowned. "No. It's strange the way it turned out. I miss John but he brought it on himself."

Raider reached for a chair. "You got any whiskey? I have a feelin' I'm gonna want a few drinks while I'm hearin' this."

She poured him a glass of brandy. He smelled her perfume when she got closer. She was a damned fine-looking woman. He could see the outline of her breasts under the robe.

The former Mrs. Sanders went back to perch on the edge of the bed. "You got out quick, Raider. You didn't see how it happened."

"Had to go," he said. "Had a buddy in trouble. I would like to thank you now for savin' my bacon back there. If you hadn't told that doctor t' get the sheriff, we might all be dead."

She touched her throat. "Yes. Well, as I was saying, things took a strange turn. You see, Franklin Jenkins hated being mayor. He resigned a month after he took office. Then John got to be mayor. Only, he worked himself to death. Just keeled over one day."

Raider winced. "Ow, that hurts."

"I guess that comes from getting what you want," Ellen replied. "Anyway, I inherited everything. I'm a rich woman now."

"Congratulations."

She smiled at him. "Would you like some more brandy?"

Raider lifted his glass. "Sure."

She refilled it and then poured herself a drink. "Anyway, I wanted to see you again, Raider. I never got to tell you how much I admired you."

He knocked back the brandy. "Yeah, is that right?"

She pouted a little. "Oh, now don't be like that. I'm paying for your services. It's all square with your agency."

"Why'd you hire me?"

"I told them you were to be my bodyguard," she replied. "And that's not far from the truth."

He shook his head. "Listen lady, the last time I hung around with you, I almost got killed."

"I am sorry. By the way, how's the wound on your hand? I heard the kid shot you."

Raider flexed his gun hand. "It's back t' normal. Wasn't much but a scratch anyway. See the scar."

She smiled. "I was wounded too, you know. But I'm better now. Would you like to see my scar?"

Raider eyed the buxom temptress. "Yeah, why not?"

She stood up and dropped her robe.

Raider felt a stirring in his body. She was shaped just the way he liked them; big, with lots of curves. Her breasts were huge.

Ellen pointed to the place where the bullet had entered her body. "There. The doctor said I was lucky. The bullet went straight through me and came out the back. Didn't hit much, I suppose."

Raider stood up. "What makes you think I'll stay?"

She came toward him, pressing her naked body against his. "Because you're a man and I don't have any clothes on. I know I'm paying you, but that's not the reason you'll stay. You want me. You wanted me before, only you were too proud to lie with

another man's wife. Well, I'm a widow now. And I want you to
stay the night with me."

"What am I s'posed t' tell the home office?"

She grabbed his crotch. "Tell them whatever you like. My
God!"

He was rock hard.

She went to work on the buttons of his fly. When she held his
cock in her hand, her body began to tremble. She pulled him
toward the bed.

Raider knew she was right about everything. He did want her.
And he was going have her. After all, the agency had assigned
him to the former Mrs. Sanders, and the big man from Arkansas
was never one to shirk his duty.

The hard-hitting, gun-slinging Pride of the Pinkertons rides solo in this action-packed series.

J.D. HARDIN'S

RAIDER

Sharpshooting Pinkertons Doc and Raider are legends in their own time, taking care of outlaws that the local sheriffs can't handle. Doc has decided to settle down and now Raider takes on the nastiest vermin the Old West has to offer single-handedly...charming the ladies along the way.

___RIVERBOAT GOLD #17	0-425-11195-4/$2.95
___WILDERNESS MANHUNT #18	0-425-11266-7/$2.95
___SINS OF THE GUNSLINGER #19	0-425-11315-9/$2.95
___BLACK HILLS TRACKDOWN #20	0-425-11399-X/$2.95
___GUNFIGHTER'S SHOWDOWN#21	0-425-11461-9/$2.95
___THE ANDERSON VALLEY	0-425-11542-9/$2.95
___SHOOT-OUT #22	
___THE YELLOWSTONE THIEVES #24	0-425-11619-0/$2.95
___THE ARKANSAS HELLRIDER #25	0-425-11650-6/$2.95
___BORDER WAR #26	0-425-11694-8/$2.95
___THE EAST TEXAS DECEPTION #27	0-425-11749-9/$2.95
___DEADLY AVENGERS #28	0-425-11786-3/$2.95
___HIGHWAY OF DEATH #29	0-425-11839-0/$2.95
___THE PINKERTON KILLERS #30	0-425-11883-5/$2.95
___TOMBSTONE TERRITORY #31	0-425-11920-3/$2.95
___MEXICAN SHOWDOWN #32	0-425-11972-6/$2.95
___THE CALIFORNIA KID #33	0-425-12011-2/$2.95
___BORDER LAW #34	0-425-12056-2/$2.95
___HANGMAN'S LAW #35 (May '90)	0-425-12097-X/$2.95

Check book(s). Fill out coupon. Send to:

BERKLEY PUBLISHING GROUP
390 Murray Hill Pkwy., Dept. B
East Rutherford, NJ 07073

NAME_____

ADDRESS_____

CITY_____

STATE_____ZIP_____

PLEASE ALLOW 6 WEEKS FOR DELIVERY.
PRICES ARE SUBJECT TO CHANGE
WITHOUT NOTICE.

POSTAGE AND HANDLING:
$1.00 for one book, 25¢ for each additional. Do not exceed $3.50.

BOOK TOTAL	$_____
POSTAGE & HANDLING	$_____
APPLICABLE SALES TAX (CA, NJ, NY, PA)	$_____
TOTAL AMOUNT DUE	$_____

PAYABLE IN US FUNDS.
(No cash orders accepted.)

208b